Also by Frances O'Roark Dowell

Dovey Coe

Where I'd Like to Be

The Secret Language of Girls

Chicken Boy

Shooting the Moon

The Kind of Friends We Used to Be

Ten Miles Past Normal

The Phineas L. MacGuire Books
(Illustrated by Preston McDaniels)

Phineas L. MacGuire . . . Erupts!

Phineas L. MacGuire . . . Gets Slimed!

Phineas L. MacGuire . . . Blasts Off!

falling in

by

Frances O'roark dowell

atheneum books for young readers

new york   london   toronto   sydney   new delhi

ATHENEUM BOOKS FOR YOUNG READERS

An imprint of Simon & Schuster Children's Publishing Division

1230 Avenue of the Americas, New York, New York 10020

This book is a work of fiction. Any references to historical events, real people, or real locales are used fictitiously. Other names, characters, places, and incidents are products of the author's imagination, and any resemblance to actual events or locales or persons, living or dead, is entirely coincidental.

Copyright © 2010 by Frances O'Roark Dowell

All rights reserved, including the right of reproduction in whole or in part in any form.

ATHENEUM BOOKS FOR YOUNG READERS is a registered trademark of Simon & Schuster, Inc.

For information about special discounts for bulk purchases, please contact Simon & Schuster Special Sales at 1-866-506-1949 or business@simonandschuster.com.

The Simon & Schuster Speakers Bureau can bring authors to your live event. For more information or to book an event, contact the Simon & Schuster Speakers Bureau at 1-866-248-3049 or visit our website at www.simonspeakers.com.

Also available in an Atheneum Books for Young Readers hardcover edition

Book design and hand-lettering by Sonia Chaghatzbanian

The text for this book is set in Adobe Caslon.

Manufactured in the United States of America

3012 OFF

First Atheneum Books for Young Readers paperback edition April 2012

10 9 8 7 6 5 4 3 2 1

The Library of Congress has cataloged the hardcover edition as follows:

Dowell, Frances O'Roark

Falling in / Frances O'Roark Dowell. — 1st ed.

p. cm.

Summary: Middle-schooler Isabelle Bean follows a mouse's squeak into a closet and falls into a parallel universe where the childrens believe she is the witch they have feared for years, finally come to devour them.

ISBN 978-1-4169-5032-5 (hardcover)

[1. Fantasy.] I. Title.

PZ7.D75455Fal 2010

[Fic]—dc22

2009010412

ISBN 978-1-4442-2205-6 (pbk)

ISBN 978-1-4169-9902-7 (eBook)

*For my brother De, who helped me make up the story
about the carnival under the family room closet,*

and for my brother Doug, who believed us

ACKNOWLEDGMENTS

The author would like to acknowledge the following people for their help with this book: Caitlyn Dlouhy, Genius, and Kiley Frank, Assistant Genius, for being, well, geniuses; Lizzy and Barbara Dee, for once again helping me find a title; Sonia Chaghatzbanian for the fabulous jacket and interior design; Alison Velea, copy editor extraordinaire; Elizabeth Blake-Linn, who made the most marvelous cover sparklies sparkle; and Trena Griffith-Hawkins' 2008–2009 Durham Academy Huskies, *Falling In*'s first audience. Thanks for listening, guys!

The author would also like to acknowledge the following members of her tribe, who are all kind, funny, and incredibly good-looking, and who manage against all odds to keep her sane enough to write books: Amy Graham, Kathryn and Tom Harris, Danielle Paul, the O'Roarks, the Dowells, the most fabulous Jonikas gals, and as always, and with big, big love, Clifton, Jack, and Will Dowell (and, of course, Travis).

There is a crack in everything,
that's how the light gets in.

~ *Leonard Cohen*

1

On the morning this story begins, Isabelle Bean was convinced she was teetering on the edge of the universe. Which is why, instead of copying spelling words off the board as instructed by Mrs. Sharpe, she had her ear pressed to her desk. All morning a strange sensation had buzzed along her fingers every time she'd put her pencil to a piece of paper, and by the time spelling period had come around, she had determined that the buzzing was coming up from the floor, through the desk's legs, and up to the desktop.

She closed her eyes in order to concentrate more fully on the buzzing. It was like the buzz that a house makes when it thinks no one's home—the refrigerator humming a little tune, the computer purring in the corner, cable lines wheezing softly as they snake through the walls and underneath the floorboards.

Being a careful listener from way back, Isabelle knew this wasn't the school buzzing. Elliot P. Hangdale Middle School never buzzed. In the mornings it rumbled and moaned as the children settled themselves into their desks and teachers cleared their throats, and in the quiet of the afternoon, students, janitors, and administrative assistants dozing off in every corner, it emitted a low-pitched whine, as though begging someone to bring it a glass of water.

So if it wasn't the school that was causing Isabelle's ear to tingle, then what? Isabelle felt if she could just hold her head still enough, for just a few seconds more, the answer would rise up from the floor and deposit itself into her brain, and maybe, finally, the floor would open up beneath her and she would fall into a far more interesting place than Mrs. Thalia Sharpe's sixth-grade classroom.

"Isabelle Bean, I've asked you a question! What is your answer, please?"

Isabelle's head jerked up and snapped back so violently she was surprised it didn't fly straight off her neck. Mrs. Sharpe's squeal of a voice always had this effect on her various limbs and appendages, as though Isabelle were a puppet and Mrs. Sharpe's high-pitched voice her master. Fortunately for Isabelle, Mrs. Sharpe's general inclination was to ignore her, but even Mrs. Sharpe couldn't ignore what appeared to be blatant napping.

"And your answer is?" Mrs. Sharpe drummed her fingers against her desk to demonstrate her impatience.

"One hundred ninety-seven?" Isabelle guessed, remembering a moment too late that it was spelling period, not math.

Her classmates twittered and giggled. One boy in particular, Ferguson Morse, was especially tickled by Isabelle's answer, and when Ferguson was tickled he began to hiccup violently. Ferguson's hiccups caused Monroe Lark to laugh so hard he rolled out of his chair and into the middle of the aisle. Within seconds, the class was in a complete uproar.

"Isabelle Bean!" Mrs. Sharpe bellowed from the front of the classroom, pointing a finger violently toward the door. "To the principal's office!"

Isabelle sighed a feather-brush sort of a sigh. Why always the same old thing? Couldn't Mrs. Sharpe come up with something more original? Why not shoot Isabelle out of a cannon, send her flying over the top of the playground's monkey bars? Why not enlist her in the Foreign Legion and deport her to deepest, darkest France?

That was the problem with adults, Isabelle thought sadly as she stood and brushed a few eraser crumbs from her lap. They lacked originality. Why, just this morning over breakfast her mother had made the most hopelessly boring suggestion that she and Isabelle should go shopping this weekend. "Janice Tribble told me there was a big sale at the mall," her mother had said, reaching across the table for the jam jar. "Twenty percent off everything at the Junior Wear Jamboree."

"You want me to go to the mall?" Isabelle could hardly believe it. The mall? Home of dreary raincoats and unnecessary sportswear? Capital of cinnamon buns that smelled wonderful, but tasted like sponges left for months under the sink? The very thought made Isabelle want to lie down and go to sleep for a hundred years.

"People do it all the time, Isabelle," her mother said in a weary voice, a V of disappointment or worry or sadness (or some heavyhearted combination of all three) appearing between her eyes. "It's quite a convenient way to purchase clothing."

"I've decided to make all my clothes from now on," Isabelle reported. The idea had burst into her head that very second, the way ideas did all the time—ideas like little constellations of sparks and light and bright colors—and she immediately liked it. So what if she didn't exactly know how to sew? So what if she had the dexterity of a webbed-toed walrus? Why should that stop her?

"Izzy, you can't even—," her mother started, then stopped. She studied the jam jar (boysenberry,

Isabelle's favorite), then carefully dolloped a blob onto her toast and spread it with the back of her spoon before cutting the toast into four little triangles. As she lifted a triangle to her mouth and began nibbling on a corner, a splotch of jam dropped on her chin, and Isabelle thought about reaching across the table to dab at it with her napkin, but decided she liked how the blob of jam looked. Like a beauty mark, she thought.

"I just remembered that I'm allergic to the mall," Isabelle said after a few moments of her mother's chewing. "But if you really want to go shopping, maybe we could go to a thrift store. That could be fun, don't you think?"

Mrs. Bean grimaced. "Hand-me-down clothes. I wore them my whole childhood. They smell like attics and old people snoring."

"Sometimes they do," Isabelle agreed. "But sometimes they don't. Besides, you can always wash them."

"The smell never goes away, no matter how many washings," Mrs. Bean said, tucking the last bit of toast in her mouth. Picking up her plate, she stood to go into the kitchen, then paused and looked back at Isabelle, her face brightening. "How about catalogs? We could order you some new things from catalogs."

Oh, what was the use? Isabelle nodded at her mother. "Sure, maybe we could do that."

Grown-ups, she thought as she grabbed her backpack to go meet the bus. The mall! Catalogs! Why couldn't they ever do something the slightest bit unusual? Unexpected?

Laziness, maybe. Or lack of imagination.

That was it: Lack of imagination.

Sometimes Isabelle dreaded growing up.

The path to Vice Principal Closky's office was a familiar route. Over the years Isabelle had demonstrated an impressive talent for irritating teachers to the extremes of their patience. It wasn't something she set out to do. In fact, she never quite understood what she did to raise her teachers' blood pressure to such dangerous levels. Neither did her teachers, and this irritated them even more. Teacher's college had equipped them to handle nose pickers, fire starters, back talkers, hitters, biters, and whiners. But quiet girls who weren't shy, girls who talked in riddles but were never actually rude, girls who simply refused to comb those confounded bangs out of their eyes, well, girls like that were beyond them.

Isabelle slowed to admire the latest crop of fifth-grader artwork hanging on the wall between Ms. Palmer and Mr. Wren's classrooms and took a moment to peer into the cafeteria, which seemed to her a more cheerful place at nine thirty in the morning than when it was overtaken by screaming kids and yellow trays still steaming from the dishwasher. Reaching the door to Vice Principal Closky's outer office, she decided a short rest was in order. She enjoyed her visits with the vice principal, but resting now would serve in the long run to delay her return to Mrs. Sharpe's classroom.

The hallway's gray linoleum felt cool beneath her legs, which Isabelle had stretched out in front of her so she could examine her boots. She'd found them the day before in a pile of junk set out for the garbage collectors. Isabelle couldn't resist picking through roadside junk, much to her mother's dismay. She'd made loads of good finds over the years, including a bike with a bent tire that had only taken two good thwacks of a hammer to restore to its proper alignment, and a goldfish, still very much alive, swimming in a goldfish bowl. Although her mother had a strict no-pets policy, Isabelle had been able to effectively argue that fish weren't pets, since you couldn't actually pet them.

The boots had been stuffed under the cushion of a crumbling Barcalounger. They were women's red leather lace-up boots, shiny and new-looking, flat heeled with surprisingly pointy toes. Isabelle's feet had grown two sizes over the past summer, and the boots fit her nicely once she'd stuffed some toilet paper in them. And while it would be hard to argue that they in any way matched her current outfit of a hooded gray sweater and loose jeans, Isabelle felt that her boots somehow completed her.

She looked up when she heard giggling voices floating down the hallway. Two girls in gym suits walked toward her—or rather, one was walking and the other was limping, her arm flung around the other girl's shoulder as if to steady herself. Isabelle recognized the limping girl as Charley Bender.

If you had to see somebody in the hallway, Charley Bender wasn't so bad, Isabelle supposed. She wasn't exactly Isabelle's cup of tea, but she was okay for the kind of girl who was usually picked third or fourth for games in PE, who stuttered a bit at the beginning of class presentations but calmed down after a minute or two and was only halfway boring on the topic of the Major Domestic Imports of Southern Lithuania.

But Isabelle had noticed that Charley Bender was one of the few people at school who said hello to Morris Kranhopf, a boy who had to wear a shoe with a special raised heel, because his left leg was shorter than his right. And so she guessed that Charley was decent for someone who was as average as an apricot.

(Were apricots average? Isabelle wondered. Better make that apples. Or acorns.)

"Is the nurse in?" Charley called to her, as though Isabelle were the receptionist. "I need her to wrap up my ankle. Gopher hole."

"Gopher hole what?" Isabelle asked. "Gopher hole who?"

"She stepped in a gopher hole, birdbrain," Charley's helper said. "She's lucky she didn't break her ankle."

Lucky, Isabelle mouthed to herself. Now that was the truth. Girls like Charley Bender were usually lucky, in her experience. Why was that? Where other people would have broken five bones in their foot, the Charley Benders of the world only twisted their ankle. They were forever reaching the doorway just as the rain began to pour from the sky, or jumping onto the curb only seconds before the speeding car rounded the corner. What fairies stood over the cradle and cast their lucky spells the day Charley Bender was born?

"So, have you seen the nurse?" Charley asked again.

"I'm not here to see the nurse," Isabelle replied.

Charley sighed. "Maybe I'll just check for myself." She poked her head into the doorway one door down from the principal's office.

"Is she there?" her friend asked. "Because Mr. Lasso said I had to get right back to class, but I guess I could wait with you if the nurse isn't there."

"Not there," Charley reported. "But I can wait by myself. I don't mind."

Not needing any further encouragement, her friend turned and trotted back down the hallway. Charley Bender disappeared into the nurse's office, and Isabelle resumed admiring her red boots.

A sudden squeak followed by a piercing squeal punctured Isabelle's reveries. Both noises came from the nurse's office. Isabelle was sure the squeal had issued forth from the mouth of Charley Bender, but where had the squeak come from?

Intrigued, she decided to investigate.

2

But first, something more about Isabelle Bean.

(What? You're ready to get on with the story? You hate it when a story gets started and then slows to a complete halt? Me too. I totally sympathize. But this will only take a second—two seconds at most—I promise. Trust me.)

You know her, of course. Isabelle Bean is the girl who sits in the back corner of the classroom near the pencil sharpener. She isn't invisible, exactly, but she might as well be. She hardly ever speaks unless spoken to (and then only in riddles), never makes eye contact, has bangs that hang down almost to her nose so even if somebody wanted to look her straight in the eye, they couldn't.

It goes without saying that very few people want to look Isabelle Bean straight in the eye.

It's not that she smells bad. She doesn't. She takes a bath every night. And it's not that she's dumb, although it's true she has a bad habit of not doing her homework except when she really feels like it, which is almost never.

And it's not that Isabelle Bean is a bully. She's never beaten anyone up or even made the smallest threat. No one is physically scared of her, except for a few of the very nice girls in Mrs. Sharpe's class, girls whose hair smells like apple blossoms and whose mothers still read them bedtime stories. These are the girls who sharpen their pencils at home so they never have to walk near Isabelle's desk.

There's a barely visible edge of otherworldliness to Isabelle, a silver thread that runs from the top of her head to the bottom bump of her spine. It frightens other children away. They're afraid that if they sit too close, the thread will weave itself into their hair and pull them into dark places they can't find their way out of. A girl named Jenna claimed it reached out to grab her one day as she walked up the aisle on her way to recess, but she had her scissors in her pocket (don't ask why) and nipped it before it could entangle her.

A girl who sits in the back corner, a girl who is as silent as a weed, a girl who everyone stays away from as though she were contagious. No friends, of course. Oh, there was that one back in second grade, the one who always came to school with yesterday's dirt still underneath her nails, but that didn't last long. The other girls stole her away. It was a game they liked to play, Keep Away from Isabelle. Rules: Leave one girl (that weird Isabelle Bean) outside so other girls (everybody else) can congratulate themselves for being inside. Old news, old news.

By the time Isabelle reached third grade, she had given up on friendship. She'd grown tired of sending birthday party invitations to children who never RSVP'd, much less appeared at her door on the given date with brightly wrapped packages in their hands. She'd given up making persimmon cookies to bring to school, where the other children called them Cootie Cookies and refused to eat them. She'd given up handing out Valentines stenciled with pictures of beating, winged hearts. She'd even given up smiling at girls who seemed shy and in need of a friend themselves.

What she never gave up: Telling herself jokes and laughing under her breath. Memorizing the letters she found in her alphabet soup and rearranging them into stories.

And she never gave up hope. She always kept a tiny sliver of it in her right pocket. Just in case it might come in handy someday.

3

Up until the moment of the squeal and the squeak, it had been a dull year for Isabelle.

Now, when it came to Isabelle and school, dull was not always bad. Dull meant you were left to yourself, generally ignored, not fully acknowledged by your classmates to exist. And there were benefits to this. When other children started paying attention to Isabelle, they often took her the wrong way.

Just the week before, Truma DeStefano had been standing behind Isabelle in the cafeteria line when she noticed a strange light snaking around Isabelle's legs. "Isabelle is wrapped up in supernatural spirits," she whispered to her best friend, Casey Weathervane, pointing to the shimmering light. "She's a ghost magnet!"

Casey, being on the high-strung side, let out a shriek that caused one of the cafeteria ladies to drop a ten-gallon pot of chili in the middle of the kitchen, which in turn provoked a swarm of swear words that the children usually only heard at home when their fathers were watching their favorite football teams blow a big game. A gaggle of lunchroom monitors came running, and Casey and Truma pointed at Isabelle's legs, where the light still hovered ominously. Isabelle stood very still, like a small animal cornered by a pack of snarling dogs.

Mrs. Wigglestaff, the most seasoned of the lunchroom monitors, sighed. "It's the light bouncing," she told the girl. She motioned to the overhead lights, then tilted her head toward the dishwasher's steel door. "Bounce, bounce, bounce," she said, her finger tracking the path of the light from ceiling to dishwasher to the spot where Isabelle just happened to be standing.

Truma and Casey giggled, but uttered not one word of apology to Isabelle, not one careless

"Whoops!" It was Isabelle Bean, after all. One did not actually direct comments toward Isabelle Bean unless one absolutely had to.

No, on the whole, Isabelle preferred her school days event free. Dull was good. Dull meant her thoughts could roam here and there, uninterrupted. But even Isabelle had to admit that sometimes dull was, well, kind of dull. A momentary interjection of a squeak and a squeal wasn't a bad thing, she decided as she poked her head into the nurse's office to see what Charley Bender was going on about.

Charley was standing on a chair in the corner. "I don't usually yell when I see mice," she said sheepishly when she saw Isabelle in the doorway. "I'm really not afraid of mice."

"But are mice afraid of you?" Isabelle walked into the room and leaned against the sink, prepared to be disappointed by Charley's reply. Girls like Charley Bender never had good answers to riddles, especially riddles that had no answers.

"I don't think this one was," Charley said. "He

looked me straight in the eye, like he wanted to say something to me, ask me a question. It sort of spooked me, if you want to know the truth."

"Of course I want to know the truth," Isabelle replied. "What else would I want to know? A trunk full of lies?"

Well, actually, now that you mention it, Isabelle didn't mind lies, as long as they were interesting lies that didn't get anyone hurt. But she suspected Charley Bender was a truth teller from way back. Charley Bender looked like a rose petal fresh from its morning bath. Rose petals were notoriously poor liars.

Hopping gingerly down from the chair and limping past Isabelle, Charley made her way to the closet on the far side of the room. "He looked at me, I yelled, and he disappeared into here. There must be a mouse hole in there or something. My dad says this is the time of year when mice start building nests inside, so they have a safe place to have their babies. There's one that lives in our attic all spring."

Isabelle came and stood next to her. "Maybe he needed a Band-Aid," she said. "Maybe he was out playing mouse soccer and fell into an ant hole."

Charley Bender rolled her eyes at Isabelle. Girls like Charley Bender were always rolling their eyes at Isabelle. It was because they never knew whether or not she was kidding. But why would she kid about mice? Why couldn't a mouse play soccer? Or paint a picture? Or start up a small business selling cheese crackers and Cat-B-Gone spray? She supposed their tails might get in the way on the soccer field, and that as a species they might not have a head for business, but that didn't push these ideas out of the realm of possibility.

Isabelle put her hand on the doorknob. "Maybe there's a whole mouse country right inside this closet, did you ever think of that? Mice families, mice swimming pools, mice courthouses where the mice go to settle their disputes."

When Charley only nodded, Isabelle continued, enjoying this riff on the life of *mus domesticus*, the beloved house mouse. "Yes, I believe I'd like to visit the country of Mice. I'll try to be back by lunch-time, but if I'm not, save one perfect french fry for me, would you?" And with that, she twisted the doorknob—

Y

I'd like to stop here for a moment, if I could. I want you to think about how many times you've opened a door. What happened? You twisted the knob, pushed or pulled, walked inside or outside, or from one room to another.

You've imagined the alternatives, though, haven't you? Or at least dreamed them? Of course you have. Everybody's had the dream where you find a door inside your house you'd never noticed before. You open it and—*whoa!*—a room you never knew existed. Usually it's filled with wondrous things, pinball machines and cakes, magnificent dollhouses, skateboard runs, a pony. There is the occasional vampire, of course, or a man in a brown suit who lacks only a head. Those are the dreams where, when you turn around, you can't find the door anymore. I hate those dreams.

If you have a little time to waste, go put your hand on the knob of the door to your room. Close your eyes and take a deep breath. What's that noise you hear? Could it be your books reading themselves to one another? Is that your goldfish whistling Mozart's *Eine Kleine Nachtmusik*? That *thump*, *thud*, *crash!*—your pillows having a pillow fight? Do you smell the earthy, froggy smell of trolls? What exactly goes on in your room when you're not around?

But I digress. Back to the story.

5

Isabelle could feel Charley Bender watching her as she pulled open the supply closet door. She could sense Charley taking a step backward, in case the residents of Mice swarmed out.

(Only later would it occur to her what a narrow escape she'd made. If Charley had stayed right where she was, if she hadn't taken that fateful backward step, she would have been able to reach Isabelle in time. Instead Charley lunged forward, arms out, desperately trying to grab a sleeve or the toe of a red boot, but she was too late.)

—and Isabelle Bean opened the door—

—and Isabelle Bean fell in.

She'd been wrong about the mice.

There'd been the tunnel—or was it a shaft? A secret passageway? Just a great big hole?—the long fall down followed by the soft tumble onto what turned out to be a pile of coats, children-sized, not mouse-sized, tree bark brown, morning gray, and mossy green, big buttons for little fingers.

Isabelle closed her eyes. She smelled mothballs tinged with licorice. She smelled dust motes and gingersnaps. She could hear the thudding of feet, voices yelling out directions, the scratching of chalk against a slate board.

She could hear the buzz.

In Mrs. Sharpe's classroom the buzz had been a

distant thing, felt more than heard. Here, wherever *here* was, the buzz flattened out into a low-pitched hum, the sound of tiny motorcycles, maybe, or an off-kilter ceiling fan endlessly running, issuing a quiet whine. Isabelle stood, determined to find its source.

A hallway stretched before her, the floor laid out in broad wooden planks, knotholes the size of fists. If this was the basement of Hangdale Middle School, it had a strange way of showing it. What sort of school basement had windows, for instance, the glass set in waves as though still vaguely liquid, the sun falling through and staining the hardwood floor with wide bars of yellow light?

Isabelle's boots tap-tapped against the floor as she made her way down the hallway, a much more satisfying sound than the thud they made when she walked across the linoleum upstairs. Upstairs? Glancing at the ceiling, she saw thick beams and rough gray plaster. Definitely not Board of Education–approved building materials.

Which caused Isabelle to wonder: Was there still

an upstairs up there? Was Charley Bender still standing at the open mouth of the closet, her hands waving, fingers wriggling, wondering where on earth Isabelle had tumbled to? Or was Charley Bender no longer there? Maybe what was up there had disappeared and there was no *there* there at all.

Next question: Was there really a *here*, or had Isabelle conked her head and was now frolicking in the land of her dreams? Was this Fairyland? The Underworld? Or just a concussion? No, Isabelle decided quickly, feeling her head for bumps and not finding any. Wherever she was, it was real. But where was she?

Eager to find out, she quickened her pace. There—an open door. Isabelle's cheeks and the tips of her fingers tingled. What if there were something fantastical inside, a dragon, say, or elves? If there were elves inside (and this is what Isabelle wished for, as she'd spent practically half her life immersed in fairy tales and fantasy books, all of them heavily populated by wonderful creatures), she hoped at least a few of them were the truly magical sort that made up long poems and lived in the high branches of trees. She couldn't stand those mealy-mouthed, cheerful elves that were always showing up in Christmas specials. Those weren't really elves, Isabelle thought. They were more like short cheerleaders in funny caps.

Her head was so filled with the variety of elves that might possibly populate the room she was about to enter that it took her a moment to see the creature who had stepped out into the hallway and now stood before her. Isabelle was taken aback, for this particular creature wasn't an elf, or an ogre, or anything fantastical whatsoever, just an ordinary girl, wearing what Isabelle supposed could be called a frock. It was made of some nubbly gray material, a plain white apron tied over it.

Isabelle stepped toward the girl, her hand raised in a half wave. "Hi, I'm—"

But before she could finish her greeting, the girl began to scream.

"It's her! It's her!" the girl caterwauled in a surprisingly loud voice for such a small child. She scurried back into the room she'd just come out of. "Run away, everyone! It's the witch, and she's come to eat us!"

7

You want me to tell you where Isabelle is, don't you? You want me to spell it out for you, draw you a map, paint a picture.

Well, I'm not going to do it. You'll have to figure it out for yourself. The girl? Maybe she's your long-lost sister, did you ever think of that? Remember all those nights you heard your mother whispering into the phone? Who did you think she was talking to? Grammy? Since when has your mother ever spoken to her mother in a whisper?

Okay, I'll tell you one thing: The girl's name is Fiona. She's five. She has very little to do with this story.

And, oh yes. She's not from here.

8

"What do you mean, she's the witch? This girl don't look nothing like a witch. Besides, the witch is old and haggard, and this girl's no older than I am."

A rough-hewn boy of thirteen or so stood in front of Isabelle, examining her. "I'll admit, I've not seen a village girl dressed as such, but you can't predict with a runaway, can you? They show up dressed every which way. I seen one in a priest's clothes once, and he weren't nothing but a lad, ten years at the very most."

"But Samuel, look at her shoes," the little girl, the screamer, who now spoke quite calmly, insisted. "Red boots are witch's shoes, I've heard Mam say it a hundred times."

A few of the other children in the circle around Isabelle murmured in agreement. Isabelle peered down at her feet. Witch's shoes? Well, yes, she had to admit, she could see that.

The boy named Samuel ran a hand through his flame red hair. "The shoes are troublesome. But let's be sensible now." He grabbed Isabelle roughly by the shoulder and turned her in a slow circle, as though he were exhibiting her. "Does she really look a witch to you? Too young, and no bloat. A child eater always has a bit of bloat around the gut, they say, for the children's souls do not digest in the way of other food."

Another boy stepped forward, this one taller, thin in the face, with a nose as sharp and pointed as a rat's. "A minion then, if not the witch, which still makes her a danger."

Isabelle stood silently. Should she defend herself? Against what? The children obviously didn't know what to make of her, and Isabelle didn't know how to explain. She could give them the long version of her life story, beginning with her birth in the backseat of the family's dented and battered Toyota Corolla, an event so traumatizing that her mother swore at the door of the emergency room that this baby would be her last. She could treat them to fun family lore. Did you know, she might ask the children, that both of my parents are orphans? That I have no grandparents, no cousins, no aunts, not one single uncle? That I am the only child of the loneliest family in the universe?

But maybe the short version of her life story would be more appropriate: Five minutes ago I fell through a closet in the nurse's office, and here I am!

Isabelle suspected that telling the children about falling through the closet wouldn't help her case. Looking around the room, with its heavy wooden tables, the black cast-iron stove hunched in the corner, the wind rasping through its small window (could that be where the buzzing hum came from?), she doubted anything about her world would make sense to these kids. There were a dozen or so of them, the youngest maybe five, the oldest one the redheaded boy named Samuel. They were clearly not of her century. Isabelle didn't keep up with fashion, cared not one whit for designer labels, but she could tell at ten paces a shirt made out of homespun cloth from one bought at a discount store. Anyone could.

And the children's faces—Isabelle found them softer than the faces of Hangdale Middle School, more open, more like flowers in the first light of day. Clearly—to Isabelle, at least—these were not faces that had spent hundreds of hours in front of television screens absorbing stories of murder and mayhem, nor were they faces that knew one gaming system from another, an Xbox from a Ybox from a Zbox.

She thought if she could get Samuel away from the other children and explain to him what had happened to her, he might understand. He looked like a pretty smart guy. There were only two problems with this plan: One, Isabelle figured it would be nearly impossible to speak to Samuel in private, and two, she wasn't sure that she wanted to explain herself. It would be nice to be a mystery for a little while longer, as long as it didn't get her beat up.

Samuel's voice broke into her thoughts. "A minion? What would a minion be doing here?" He stepped away from Isabelle, as if to get a better angle on her. "The witch is done with us for now and won't be back this way any time soon. We're out of season. Surely she'd send no minions here."

The rat-faced boy shrugged. "Better not to take a chance. Da says the crops were bad in Corrin this year; maybe the littlest ones there have grown thin. She likes 'em fat, I hear. They go down better with a little meat on 'em."

A small girl, five at most, began to cry. Isabelle's eyes widened. Was this kid afraid of her? She turned away from Samuel and toward the others.

"Good people," she said, holding out her hands as if to prove she carried no weapons. "Listen to me. I am not a witch."

She stopped. Her voice sounded strange, like she was doing a bad imitation of herself or acting in a play written by tin-eared third graders. And since when had she ever used the phrase "good people"? If a rewind button had been available to her, she would have held it down for twenty seconds and started over.

Instead she continued, "I can't prove to you I'm not a witch. I also can't prove to you I'm not a genie or a werewolf or the starting pitcher for the Boston Red Sox."

"Eh?" Samuel looked at her quizzically.

Deep breath. Start again.

"I'm a girl. I'm not sure where I am. But I am sure who I am, and who I am not is a witch."

Now all the kids looked at her like she was crazy. Of course, Isabelle was used to this, so she didn't take it personally. She noticed Samuel and Rat Face exchanging glances, sending each other secret messages across the room, making a plan. Suddenly Samuel's hand was clamped around her wrist.

"I think you best be off, then," he said, pulling her toward the doorway. "Though I don't believe you to be a witch, we'll not take any chances. If you're a runaway, well, there's no more room in the village for runaways. Now that the witch is outside of Corrin, we're packed to the brim with all the children trying to escape. I suggest you make for the woods; there'll be camps out there, closer to Drumanoo and such places."

Isabelle felt herself propelled out the door and back into the wide hallway. Samuel stepped out from behind her and pointed her in the direction of a heavy door at the end of the hall. "You go through that door and follow the path to the village. When it forks, you'll go to the right, to the woods. Follow the creek north and you'll find the camps in an hour's walk. South will take you to Corrin. You'll want to stay as far from Corrin as you can, lest you cross paths with the witch."

The air outside was warm for early April, and Isabelle wondered if it was, in fact, April air, or if she'd entered not just another world, but another season, too.

She followed the path into the woods, which were cool and inviting, the gnarled trees heavy with leaves, branches arching in a canopy over her head. So what were these camps Samuel had been talking about? She didn't want to go to a camp, especially not a camp filled with children. She knew about children. If they smelled the merest molecule of something different about you, noticed that one of your ears was set higher than the other, discovered disturbing patterns in the freckles on your arms—a wolf here, a pig's head there—they turned against you. They made up stories about you. Watch out for that girl, they'd say, she morphs into a zombie whenever there's a full moon. Do you see that girl? they'd ask. She squashes mosquitoes on her arms and licks up the blood.

No, camps full of children were not for her. But a witch?

Isabelle would really like to meet a witch.

When she reached the creek, she headed south.

9

Isabelle Bean had always wondered if she was, in fact, a changeling—

10

You've probably guessed that about her already, haven't you? Yes, Isabelle thought she was a changeling. Or at least believed there was a strong possibility she was a changeling. Okay: She had no proof whatsoever that she was a changeling, but she really, really hoped it was true.

You know about changelings, right? Please don't tell me you go to one of those schools where they only teach things you can actually prove, like two plus two equals the capitol of Arizona. Do you hear me sighing? I want you to march into your principal's office first thing in the morning and say, "I demand you educate my imagination!" Homeschooled? Tell it to your mom.

There are changelings everywhere. Most bullies are changelings, but a lot of shy children are too. That kid who's always tripping over his own two feet? Definitely a changeling.

Here's the deal: One day a beautiful, perfect baby is born, and his mom and dad make a huge fuss, take a gazillion pictures on their cell phones and post them to their website, www.ourbabyisbetterthanyours.com, and generally behave like they're the only people in the world who ever had a cute kid. Big mistake. There are fairies flitting all around your average maternity ward just waiting for that kind of hubris. The minute the parents turn their backs, watch out! A fairy trades out Little Miss Beautiful Baby for Little Miss Cross-Eyed. Happens all the time.

Except sometimes the fairies make mistakes. They trade out Little Miss Beautiful for Little Miss Magical. Sometimes in their haste they grab an elf baby and trade that. Now, elf babies aren't much to look at, it's true, and they grow into plain, unexceptional-seeming children, but there comes a day, right around their twelfth birthdays, when they blossom like lilies. You know who I'm talking about, don't you? The ugly duckling of the sixth grade who turns into the beautiful swan of seventh grade? Elf baby. Skinny kid turned Adonis? Elf baby.

There are changelings all around you. If you'd been receiving a proper education all these years, you'd know that.

11

—and as she walked the path south toward Corrin, Isabelle pondered the notion again. She poked at it and played with it. A changeling! It would explain so much! Why she never understood the games other children played, could never get the hang of tag, flailed and flopped at kickball, never once scooped up a jack, then snatched the little red ball out of the air. Marbles skittered away from her. Jump ropes? No need to discuss.

But Isabelle had other powers, or so she believed, powers normal children didn't possess. She could make the second hand of a clock tick forward two tocks instead of one just by staring at it with her right eye, her left eye closed. Twice she'd made it snow by crushing five ice cubes and laying their remains on her windowsill at night. Moreover, she was fairly certain she and a squirrel who lived in her yard were in cahoots. She whistled, the squirrel tilted his head and chattered back. This had happened three times. The squirrel looked as if he knew Isabelle from somewhere else, and maybe he did. From the Enchanted Forest, Isabelle thought, the Other World, or maybe the Land of the Elves—whatever faraway place she had originally come from.

She looked into the trees, half expecting to see her squirrel looking back at her now, but there were no squirrels to be seen, at least not on this part of the path. A few birds chattered behind the bushes, and the creek muttered absentmindedly as it wound its way through the woods. Maybe, thought Isabelle, the squirrels were at lunch.

A changeling. The daughter of a fairy, or maybe a troll, although Isabelle hoped not a troll. True, she had a bad temper, as trolls were known to, and she supposed a troll could have tired of her at an early age and traded her in for some other child, a sweeter, prettier girl. Still, she'd rather be the offspring of an elf. Authentic elves were beautiful, if a little bit on the silly side. Isabelle wasn't beautiful, she knew, but maybe one day she would be. Sometimes her mother brushed her hair out of her eyes and said, "You never know, Izzy. You could really be something when you grow up," her voice only half-doubtful.

If Isabelle was a changeling and was now on a journey back to her true home, she wondered if another girl, the one stolen from the crib in her mom's house and replaced by Isabelle—was right now making her way back to *her* true home. If so, Isabelle felt sorry for her.

It wasn't that her mother was so bad. She tried, but she'd had no training, and when Isabelle's dad had left after her third birthday, Mrs. Bean (much to her dismay) had had to do duty as a single parent, feeling more clueless than ever.

The fact was, Isabelle's mom hadn't known the simplest thing about making a home for a kid. She didn't know that children need bright colors and happy music, or that they should be read to every single day, fairy tales and folktales, funny books about trucks and silly books about cats wearing hats. From what Mrs. Bean had read in the newspapers, she assumed that television was the best way to keep a girl entertained, and so a gigantic, flat-screened monster of a TV was planted in the center of the living room, always on, always yakking away. Isabelle ignored it to the best of her ability.

A quilt and a pair of flouncy curtains that hung over Isabelle's window, both hand-me-downs from one of her mother's coworkers, were the only splashes of color in an otherwise dreary house. "Someone has to teach you how to decorate, and no one ever taught me," her mom said from time to time, apropos of nothing. She might be packing Isabelle's lunch or polishing her reading glasses on the sleeve of her sweater. It was as if every so often Mrs. Bean found herself in the middle of an argument with an invisible critic. "I grew up in an orphanage, you know. I didn't have a mother to tell me what sort of things to hang on the wall."

So the walls of the Beans' house remained bare of paintings and photographs. And no one ever got upset about a vase being broken by an errant baseball, because there were no vases, or any potted plants, ceramic ashtrays, glass figurines, antique lamps, or gilt-framed mirrors for a baseball to demolish.

But Isabelle had never minded. Her imagination was so lavishly decorated she didn't need inspiration from framed prints and hand-painted pillows. She had only minded the dark, especially in the winter months, when the days ended early, finding Isabelle alone in the house, the light slipping out the windows.

Now she wished she'd had time to leave a note before she'd left home. *You'll find my books in a pile in my closet,* she'd have written. *Please let your real daughter read them! Also: The bathrooms should be painted another color. Industrial gray is depressing! And buy more fruit! Children need fruit!*

The thought of strawberries and bananas made Isabelle hungry. She hadn't eaten since breakfast, and then only half an English muffin with a dab of apple butter. Her stomach had felt funny that morning, and now Isabelle wondered if she hadn't somehow known that today was the day when she'd be returned to her true home.

A large, smooth rock, the size and the shape of a beanbag chair, presented itself in the middle of the path, and Isabelle sat down on it. If she didn't eat something soon, she'd get a pinched feeling between her eyes, a feeling that could only be gotten rid of by taking two headache pills and placing an ice pack on her forehead for thirty minutes. If the headache wasn't treated immediately, the pain grew larger and began to squeeze Isabelle's head from either side, as if Isabelle were an orange and somebody wanted a glass of juice. Isabelle needed to eat.

She closed her eyes and held out her hands. If this were an enchanted forest, as Isabelle hoped it was, then maybe all she had to do was wish for food. *Don't be greedy,* she told herself as she composed her lunch order. A little cup of blueberries would do nicely, as would a turkey sandwich—though, did they serve turkey sandwiches in enchanted forests? Turkey sandwiches seemed so . . . unenchanted. A dripping honeycomb, that's what she should wish for, though Isabelle didn't really like honey, except in tea. Too sticky sweet.

Porridge! A steaming bowl of porridge! Of course. The exact right thing. Isabelle lifted her hands a little higher and wished for a bowl of porridge, not knowing if she should wish out loud, so she didn't.

She waited to feel the weight of the bowl in her hands. After a few seconds, her hands still empty, she opened her eyes. A girl, no more than eight or nine, stood in front of her.

"Yes?" Isabelle asked, trying not to sound impatient even as the hunger gnawed at her belly. "What do you have for me?"

The girl stepped back, shaking her head, her eyes wide with fright. "I don't have nothing for ya, miss. Begging your pardon, miss."

"That would mean you have something," Isabelle pointed out. Was this girl a fairy, trained to speak in riddles and double negatives? She looked a little grubby and plump for a fairy, her cheeks altogether too tear streaked, but still, you never knew. "If you don't have nothing, that means you have something."

The girl straightened and took a deep breath. "I have two loaves of bread with butter what Mam gave me for the journey," she said, presenting a small burlap bag for Isabelle's view. "I'll share of 'em if you'll walk with me."

Isabelle searched her imagination for stories about fairies who shared food or took journeys, but couldn't find any. "Walk to where?"

"The camps in the woods," the girl replied. "Where the other children from Corrin went. We was walking on our way this morning when I had to stop a moment to—" She nodded toward the ground, and Isabelle understood that the girl had needed to relieve herself. "I like a private moment for that, you understand, so I went deep into the wood, and when I got out the others had gotten too far ahead. I couldn't catch up. I called after them, but no one called back."

The girl took a step closer to Isabelle. "I don't know how they could've gotten so far ahead, miss," she said in a near whisper. "Made me wonder, maybe the witch was nearby, not so far south as they say. Maybe she'd been following us and eaten them what had gone ahead of me."

Maybe, Isabelle thought, but more likely they'd run off, knowing that the girl would be scared to find herself alone. They'd heard her calls and covered their mouths so their laughter wouldn't leak out.

"I'm afraid to go on by myself, miss," the girl continued. "I'll offer my bread if you'll be my companion."

Isabelle's stomach grumbled. The pain began between her eyes. It would only be a moment before it sharpened its needlelike claws and took hold. She had to eat, but she didn't want to head north, toward the camps, away from the witch. She could walk with the girl for the time it took to eat the bread, and then she could turn back, she guessed. The path was clear; the girl wouldn't have any trouble following it.

She looked at the girl, whose lower lip was trembling. It seemed a shame to send her back to the kids who'd abandoned her. Isabelle knew about children. She knew tears wouldn't make them any nicer. Just the opposite, as a matter of fact.

Isabelle felt a soft place open inside her. She wanted to help the girl. But if the girl knew where Isabelle was headed, she'd run fast in the other direction. So Isabelle would have to be a little bit crafty about it. It was the right thing to do. What this girl needed most of all, Isabelle could clearly see, was a friend.

And so Isabelle Bean decided to give friendship one more try.

"I'll walk you to the camps." Isabelle stood and pointed south. "For a loaf of bread, and any blueberries you might have on you."

"I've not got blueberries, miss, they're not in season. But to my bread you're welcome." The girl gave Isabelle a worried glance. "Though shouldn't we start out the other way, miss?"

Isabelle touched the girl on the shoulder. "I know a shortcut," she lied.

The girl pulled a loaf of bread from her pouch and handed it to Isabelle. Isabelle broke off a piece for her young companion before shoving some into her own mouth. The pain between her eyes receded. The two of them began to walk.

12

The girl's name was Hen, and she was useful.

At first she couldn't stop worrying aloud about when the path would split and she and Isabelle would begin to make their way north. "We've been south-bound for some time now, miss," she'd noted after they'd been walking for more than an hour. "Isn't it time we broke from the path and changed direction?"

"If we keep going south, sooner or later we'll be going north," Isabelle pointed out. "One way always becomes the other if you give it time."

She could tell this bit of navigational wisdom didn't ease Hen's mind and decided to take a different approach. "Would you like me to tell you a story while we walk?"

Looking interested, the girl nodded.

"Do you know about changelings?"

Hen nodded again. "Of course, miss."

Now it was Isabelle's turn to be interested. She'd never met anyone before who knew about changelings. The kids she went to school with knew about aliens and they knew about murderers and kidnappers. They knew a little about monsters, though nothing useful, and a touch of vampire lore. But when it came to fairies, elves, changelings, and boggarts, no one Isabelle knew had the slightest idea. It seemed the most interesting things in the world were currently out of fashion.

Isabelle peered at Hen with more curiosity than she'd possessed a moment ago. "So, what exactly do you know?"

The girl laughed. "Why, all there is to know, I suppose, miss. The three Teague boys, all of them were changelings, now, weren't they? Beautiful babes their mother had each time, and then the jealous fairies stole them, and look what she got in their stead—them barrel-faced boys thumping and clumping around, no sense in 'em. Changelings, every one."

So instead of Isabelle telling stories to the girl— Hen, she said her name was, not short for anything, just Hen—the girl told stories to Isabelle, and in this way they walked for another hour, before Hen noticed that the sky was beginning to darken.

"It won't do to keep traveling, miss," she said, moving off the path and crouching beside a tree, hands on her knees. "Dark falls fast in these woods."

Isabelle hadn't thought about night coming on. In the same way that she hadn't worried about food until she got hungry, it hadn't occurred to her that she would need to sleep until nighttime crept into view. She guessed it made sense that she would, but how do you sleep if you don't have a bed? No sleeping bag? No pillow, no blanket, not the thinnest of quilts to come between you and the ground? And, come to think of it, no ceiling to come between you and the clouds?

Hen seemed to sense Isabelle's concern. "Not to

worry, miss. I'll make us a comfortable sleeping spot. I'm not good at much, but I'm good at setting up camp. If you'll help me gather a thing or two before evening comes, we'll get a good night's sleep, save the witch don't get us."

They entered the woods through a thin stand of trees. Hen told Isabelle to gather leaves while she went in search of vines and fallen branches. "You'll need more than that, miss, if you want to have a good night," Hen had chided her the first time Isabelle appeared with her arms only half full. Isabelle dumped the leaves where Hen told her to and went back for more. Soon there was a hump-backed mound at the edge of the woods. "We'll make us a bed fit for queens out of that, miss," Hen said, and Isabelle felt oddly pleased.

While Isabelle collected more leaves, Hen built a lean-to out of sticks and vines against the trunk of a chestnut tree. She showed Isabelle how to pull live branches from young maples and sycamores, leaves still firmly attached, and lay them on top of the lean-to to make a roof. "It'll be snug in there, you'll see, miss," Hen assured her. "And them leaves will make a good, green blanket."

Only a thin strip of light still lay on the horizon. "We should get water from the creek before we eat our bread rather than after," Hen said. "In five minutes, there'll be no light left for us to find our way back to camp."

Isabelle marveled at the girl. That Hen! So practical! So full of good ideas! She followed Hen to the creek and dipped her hands into the cold water. She gulped it greedily. How long had they walked? She'd been on the path at least two hours before meeting Hen, and they'd walked a good two hours after that. Four hours of walking. Isabelle smiled. Not bad for a girl who routinely got a cramp in her side after one lap around the track in PE.

The bread they ate for dinner tasted twice as delicious as it had at lunch. "I guess we should save some for morning, shouldn't we?" Isabelle asked regretfully. She could have eaten her portion and Hen's and four more loaves besides.

"I'd say so, miss," Hen replied, sweeping the

crumbs from her lap. "I don't know how far we are from the camps, but the journey will seem twice as long if we don't start off with a bit of something to eat."

"Hen?" Isabelle leaned toward the girl. "Would it surprise you to know I don't know what the camps are—or why the camps are?"

Hen smiled a rueful smile. "It wouldn't surprise me if you didn't know *where* the camps are, that's the truth of it."

Isabelle lowered her voice to a confidential whisper. "I'm not from here, Hen, and that's the truth of it too."

It was as if Isabelle had just realized this very fact herself, as if the thought—*I'm not from here*—had only now occurred to her. She'd felt at home all day, wandering down the path that split the woods, all sorts of nice smells and sounds popping up everywhere, pine and lilac and cedar and honeysuckle; birds chirping, water splashing over rocks. She felt as though she'd been sent on the best field trip in the world. Maybe not her world—or maybe it was her world?

Isabelle looked around and wondered again, *Where am I? And where is everyone else? Has Charley Bender gone back to PE? Is she at home in bed thinking over the day, explaining to herself again and again what happened? Are the authorities involved? Has my mother submitted a missing person's report?*

Isabelle found that the more she let her thoughts wander in this direction, the fuzzier her immediate surroundings became. Two thoughts about her mom phoning the police and Hen became unfocused around the edges. A little snippet of worry about Charley Bender in the principal's office trying to explain what had happened, and the shadows beneath the trees deepened into an inky black. Could she worry herself into nothingness?

It was decided, then. She wouldn't worry. Because Isabelle liked to think things happened for a reason, she decided there must be a reason she was here at the edge of this green and sweet-smelling forest chatting with the interesting and somewhat unusual Hen. She'd learn more, she was sure, as the days went by, about where she was and why. Maybe a bird would whisper the news in her left ear. Anything was possible, or at least that's what Isabelle hoped.

Hen stretched, then propped herself on her elbows. "I guessed as much that you wasn't from here, miss. Just by your clothes. If you don't mind me saying so, they're a bit odd for these parts. Are ya from Aghadoc? I've heard tell that folks from Aghadoc go about things different."

"I'm from somewhere else," Isabelle said. "If we could just leave it at that."

Hen nodded. "Everybody's from somewhere else these days, seems like. Me too, I suppose." She took a quick swipe at her eyes with the back of her arm. "I couldn't believe it when the signs came. Ignored them at first, we did. And then last night, a shadow crossed the moon, and Mam pushed me and the little ones out the door."

"And the other kids in your village got pushed out of their doors too?"

"It's our season, ya see," Hen said. "The witch's season. She's come to us now, to eat all the babies and hang the children from nets in the trees around her house, starving 'em until they're nothing but bones clattering in the night when the wind blows."

The night air fell around Isabelle's shoulders, and she pulled her hands inside the sleeves of her sweater to keep them warm. "Why does she do it?"

"Some children killed her baby," Hen answered, and gave a great shiver before she continued. "Years and years ago, when they used to have the summer festival, and all the five villages gathered. The witch lived in the woods outside of Drumanoo then, and folks left her alone. But then word came she'd had a baby, and that it was the devil's child. A group of 'em—one child from each village— snuck into the woods that night to see Satan's spawn for themselves. It was out there in the yard—in the middle of the night!—sleeping in a sling tied between two trees. One boy threw a rock at it, and then the others did, and the baby bled something fierce—"

"And it died," Isabelle finished, her voice barely

a whisper. "That's a terrible story. That's the worst story I ever heard."

Hen shook her head violently. "No! What's worse is now. She chases us from our villages. She eats our babies! She won't ever stop seeking revenge, and it's been near fifty years! I didn't kill her baby. I'd nothing to do with it."

Isabelle leaned her head back and stared up at a sky carpeted with stars. A metallic taste filled her mouth. This story—Hen's story—was taking her somewhere she didn't want to go. It had a witch, and Isabelle had always loved stories with witches in them, would check out any book from the library that had the barest hint of a witch in it. But the story also held a baby close to its heart, and Isabelle couldn't bear that baby. She couldn't bear it! Because she could see it as it had been, its little chest rising and falling as its sling swung in the night breeze, the moonlit air warm on its skin. And then—awful, awful—she could see what it became when it was no longer a baby but had become a small, lifeless body, bruises like black flowers across its arms and legs and forehead.

Hen had been right: Out of the leaves, they had made a bed fit for queens. But that night, Isabelle tossed and turned and didn't sleep until the singing of the birds lifted up the sun.

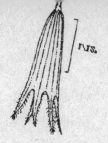

13

Let me pause here for a moment. There's a boy there in the third row, halfway back, who's had his hand in the air for the last ten minutes. I guess some of you have never heard about keeping your hands down until the person telling the story is done. Not that it's distracting to have someone waving wildly at you while you're trying to remember exact details, the order of events, what this person said to that person. Oh, no, not distracting *at all*.

You want to know what the lamps are? Oh, the *camps*. You want to know what the camps are. Haven't I explained the camps yet? I thought I had.

Here's what I know. Back in the time of the witch, in the County of the Five Villages, each village had its season, and the children of that village had to leave until the witch had moved on. (The order of the villages went Greenan, Aghadoc, Corrin, Stoneybatter, and Drumanoo.) If you lived in Corrin, you ran to the woods north of Greenan. Aghadoc—the woods south of Stoneybatter. And so on.

I don't know much about the camps, to tell you the truth. I guess if it was spring or summer the children foraged for berries, fished in the creek, threw rocks at squirrels (*not* nice, I know, but they were hungry, and it's not as if there was a grocery store half a mile down the road). Did they tell one another stories at night? Weave potholders out of long grasses? Make boats out of twigs? I don't know. Somebody else will have to tell that story. Maybe you could do it. Some of those children are still around. Oh, they're grown up now, but believe me, they haven't forgotten. Go ask them yourselves. All you have to do is find the door.

14

In the morning the two girls continued south, and Hen made no complaint. *She must know we're getting closer to the witch, not farther away,* Isabelle thought, *so why doesn't she turn around?* Maybe Isabelle should offer to turn around herself, take Hen to the camps. It would be almost a day's walk, but what was that to Isabelle? When they reached the camps, she could get more bread, maybe a jar of peanut butter—no, no, they wouldn't have that—a handful of dried apples, then, enough to survive on as she made her way back south after making sure Hen was safe in the camps.

Isabelle's eyes felt hot and scratchy, her legs as though they'd been cast in lead. She didn't have half a day's walk in her, that was the problem with her plan. Besides, there was that look on Hen's face, serious and slightly grim, as if she'd been setting her own plans in concrete all morning.

"Is this the path you walked on yesterday?" Isabelle asked, trying to make conversation. Hen's silence was beginning to worry her. "I mean, as you headed north from Corrin."

"No, miss," Hen replied. "We went through the woods. Didn't want to be out in the open, ripe for the picking, especially with a shadow moon overhead. Even a half-masked moon sheds light if it's full."

It was the sort of morning that made Isabelle happy not to be in school, the sky a soft blue, the sun warm on her shoulders but not burning. Although it hadn't rained in the night, everything around her looked freshly washed. The dirt beneath her feet was as fine as powder; in fact, Isabelle could imagine mixing it with boiling water to make hot chocolate, throwing in a few choice white pebbles for marshmallows.

There had been dirt like this at Isabelle's elementary school. She could almost feel it sifting through her fingers as she remembered all those recesses she'd spent digging and stirring, adding water, creating a world out of the milky brown muck. She'd dug a hole six inches deep and twelve inches across in a spot behind the cafeteria Dumpster and lined it with small rocks to make a sort of mixing bowl. She'd used sticks for spoons, sometimes brought a plastic knife from home, sometimes a handful of marbles to decorate the cakes and pies she made.

Kindergarten, first grade, second grade, third grade. Each year she'd rediscovered the dirt, some years in September, other years not until spring. In second grade a new girl had joined her, and for the first time Isabelle had known the pleasure of companionship, the two girls murmuring to each other as they stirred the batter for muffins or fashioned dolls from sticks and clay. A few words here and there. They hadn't needed many.

Angel Fisher. Isabelle had thought that was the most wonderful name in the world, had drawn picture after picture of a girl sitting by the edge of a stream with a net strung from silk, pulling angels out of the water. She'd mailed them to Angel using Christmas stamps. Angel had loved the dirt as much as Isabelle, had understood that it had magical properties, had understood without being told that you should never use a word like "mud" when you had the word "clay" at your disposal. Angel with her dark hair always captured in a braid, her fingernails bitten to the quick.

They'd stolen her, of course. Isabelle saw it happening. The day Angel had arrived at the dirt with a foil-wrapped chocolate kiss in her hand, her eyes wide with surprise, Isabelle knew it was only a matter of time. *April gave this to* me, Angel had said. *Right out of the clear blue sky, she gave it to* me. April Hennessey, with her yellow hair and pink skin, her nose turned up like a pig's. April, who did not want Angel's friendship, only Isabelle's misery.

"I'm going to kill her, miss."

Isabelle stopped short, scattering pebbles to the edges of the path. "Going to kill who, Hen?"

"The witch, miss," Hen replied without breaking step. "I think God sent you to lead me to her. Could it be more clear, you there waiting for me on a rock in the middle of the path? Like the Lord himself had set you down."

"How old are you, Hen?" Isabelle scrambled to catch up with the girl.

"Nine, miss. Ten in three months' time."

"Do you really think you could kill a witch? You don't have any weapons, any magic."

Hen came to a halt. "I've got strong hands, miss, strong enough to choke an old hag," she said, squeezing one hand around the other wrist as if to prove her strength. "The witch must be ancient by now, nothing more than a bundle of twigs wrapped in skin. It came to me last night, as I was falling asleep. I was thinking how weary I am of being frightened. Now it's the witch's season in Corrin, and then she'll hunt the children in Stoneybatter, and it will go on like that, village by village, round and round, until she dies. A witch can live two hundred years or more. So there's years left of it, unless she's stopped."

Hen turned and looked at Isabelle. She was quiet a moment before she spoke again. "You could help me, miss."

"Help?" Isabelle blinked several times.

"Yes, miss. You could hold her while I have my hands around her neck."

Isabelle started down the path again. The sun flared above the trees, and a squirrel perched on a tree stump chattered angrily at the acorn in its hands. Isabelle's hands began to sweat. She shoved them in her pockets.

"I didn't mean to offend, miss," Hen called breathlessly as she ran to catch up. "We'll say no more about it."

"I'm thirsty," Isabelle said. "Are you thirsty? Are we far from the creek?"

Hen looked toward the woods, her head cocked. "I don't hear the water, miss, but it can't be more than half a mile in, I wouldn't think. The creek twists and turns, but these woods aren't wide, and its course runs through the middle."

The shade of the trees cooled Isabelle's skin. As

she followed Hen, she tried to calm down. No one was going to get killed, she repeated to herself, not if she had anything to do about it. She concentrated on her breathing, thought about the way her toes flattened against the soles of her boots as she walked, how her knees bent slightly, then straightened with every step, and her arms swung loosely from her shoulders. She could feel the air finding its way between her fingers, could feel her ears holding on to her head for dear life. Every part of her hung together just so. She'd never known this about herself before. It was, well, comforting.

When a second later her foot got caught under a tree's exposed roots and Isabelle went flying, it was, well, less comforting. *Just when you're starting to get used to yourself,* Isabelle thought as she tumbled to the earth, small rocks and twigs making themselves at home in her palms, her ankle throbbing with sharp little bleats of pain.

Hen was beside her in an instant, unlacing Isabelle's red boot, pulling it from her foot. Her cool fingers felt the tender swelling. "I don't think it's broken, miss, but it might be sprained. The creek's not but a hundred yards away. You'd do well to soak your ankle in it, see if the swelling won't go down."

Isabelle leaned against Hen as she hopped on one foot toward the edge of the creek. She lay back against the mossy bank, her eyes closed, and gingerly lowered her foot into the cold water.

"You'll need to wrap that before you put your weight on it again," a voice announced from behind her. "Else you'll stretch out farther what holds it together, and it won't heal for an age and a half."

Hen was fast on her feet, scanning between the trees. "Who said that?" She leaned down to grab a large stick from the ground. "Ya best show yourself."

"You've nothing to be afraid of," a woman's voice said, and a second later, the woman herself stood in front of them, a basket dangling from her arm. "It's my woods you're in, so you are the trespassers here. But you're welcome nevertheless."

She turned to Isabelle. "Shall I take a look, then?" She nodded toward Isabelle's ankle. "I might be able to help."

Isabelle nodded. The woman had a pleasant face, lightly lined, crow's-feet at the corners of her eyes, which were blue, as in cornflower blue, as in the blue of a midsummer sky. When she leaned down to examine Isabelle, Isabelle could hear her knees crack, and thought of her mom, who seemed to crack and pop with every twist and turn of her body.

The woman held Isabelle's foot with one hand and with the other pushed it a little to the left, then a little to the right. Isabelle grimaced, and the woman raised her eyebrow. "That hurts, eh? I'd say you've got a mean sprain, but no worse. You shouldn't put your weight on it for a day or two. I can put a plaster on it. Eucalyptus leaves, camphor. To help the healing."

Hen kneeled next to Isabelle. "I've heard eucalyptus will help with a sprain."

The woman looked at her. "You know about healing, do ya?"

"Some," Hen replied. "My uncle trained to be an apothecary, but he was killed in the Nine Years' War and never put his learning to use. He taught me some things before he left."

"'Twas a bad war, that," the woman said, nodding. She stood and brushed dirt from her apron. "Took many a life, and for naught, I'd say. Kings' wars fought by villagers' sons. Folly, all of it."

The woman lifted her apron and with one motion tore a strip from near the hem, and then another. "That should do for a binding, for now at least," she said. "My house isn't but a quarter of a league from here, but you shouldn't cover any ground until that ankle is wrapped tight."

It felt natural to Isabelle to lean against the old woman's shoulder. She hopped awkwardly along on her good foot but didn't feel awkward at all. Why was that? And why did these woods seem so familiar? Why, when they got closer to the woman's house—she pointed to the smoke curling out of the chimney—did Isabelle feel like she was going someplace she'd been before?

Oh, she was pretty sure she knew why.

Well, almost sure.

Anyway, she was sure enough to start giggling like crazy, and after a minute Hen joined in, and even the old woman cracked a smile.

"Why are we laughing, miss?" Hen asked after another minute.

Isabelle shook her head. "Just happy, I guess," she said, and then it was Hen's turn to shake her head.

"Just happy," Hen repeated. "Who ever heard of such a thing?"

And then the two girls laughed some more.

Snakeroot (Polygala senega)

Take for wheezing lungs, aching noggins, and bothersome stomachs.

15

Grete's cottage was small, and it was made to seem smaller still by a cacophony of—well, the only word that Isabelle could think of was *stuff*. There was furniture, of course, but not a lot of it, a round kitchen table with two chairs next to the stove, three rocking chairs in front of the fireplace. In the small bedroom off the kitchen, there was a narrow bed and a blue washbasin on a wooden stand.

What filled the rooms of Grete's cottage so decidedly were woven baskets and wooden boxes and clay pots glazed in red and blue, each with its own mishmash of this and that. Roots and leaves still redolent of dirt. Balls of scratchy wool in variegated strands—purple twining into pink easing into periwinkle fading into gray. At least three boxes held squares and strips of fabrics, all colors, and eight pots overflowed with apples.

The walls were lined with shelves, the shelves were lined with books. Wordless spines peered out. As soon as Isabelle saw them, she itched to open one up and read it from cover to cover.

"You girls sit, and I'll bring you something to drink before I set to work on that ankle," Grete instructed as she opened the stove door and livened up the fire with a few pokes of a stick.

"Tea?" Hen asked hopefully, taking a seat at the round table.

"Of a sort," Grete replied. "And some bread, if you're hungry. I made salt bread this morning."

Isabelle thought of the salt and flour clay she'd made when she was little, the way it tasted like the ocean when she'd put a pinch of it in her mouth. But Grete's bread had sweet notes beneath the salty ones, as though the ocean had chewed on sugar cubes for breakfast. The tea, however, was bitter, and Isabelle and Hen had to stir spoonfuls of honey into their cups before they could take a single sip.

"It will make you sleepy," Grete said, pulling a rocking chair to the table and lifting Isabelle's ankle onto her lap. "You look like a girl who needs a rest. You as well, Hen."

Already Isabelle felt drowsy, but she still couldn't help wondering, had Hen told Grete her name? They hadn't introduced themselves as they'd walked through the woods to the cottage, no *How do you do's* or a single *Pleased to meet you, my name's* ———. But when they'd arrived at the doorstep, a package wrapped in rough brown paper and tied with twine was waiting, *Grete of the Woods* scrawled on it in ink so wet that it had branched out from every letter like veins. The address looked like something a spider might have written.

"That's me," Grete had said, picking up the package. "Though any more than one name is too many. The more names upon your head, the more they think they know about you."

"Who's *they?*" Hen had asked, but Grete just shook her head and said nothing more about it.

Now she carefully wrapped Isabelle's ankle with a long piece of soft fabric that smelled like cedar chips and peppermint. Isabelle felt her eyes grow heavy as Grete explained to Hen how she'd prepared the poultice, boiling eucalyptus leaves into a syrup, mixing it with wax to make a salve, then spreading the salve onto the strips of cloth.

"We'll put her in the bed, then," Isabelle heard Grete say to Hen when she'd finished, and then had the sensation of being lifted and carried through the air. Suddenly she was on something soft, an ocean maybe, a loaf of salt bread for her pillow, a bluebird singing to her across the water.

16

As I write this, there's a spider on my wall, and it's tempting to reach out and smash it. But there are things to be learned from spending time with Grete. Spiders, it turns out, are beneficial creatures in more ways than you might imagine. They capture insects you want nothing to do with, sowbugs and locusts, black flies, aphids. But more than that. Spiders are the brilliant artists of the morning. They are known to be thinkers and philosophers of the highest order. It was a spider who first understood the moon and its dance with the tides, who whispered the truth of gravity's secrets to anyone who would listen.

And that plain brown spider the size of a button on my wall? A teller of jokes, perhaps. One of the famous farmer spiders who grow tiny strawberries beneath the ferns by the side of the house. If I smashed him, what would I gain? And what might the world lose?

You could think about that the next time you're tempted to stomp an ant on the sidewalk (ants, Grete would tell you, are the noblest of creatures, loyal to their families, hard workers, and also quite funny if you catch them in that moment just before sunset, their hauling and building done for the day, their frantic pace finally slowed) or are motivated to capture a butterfly and pin it to a piece of cardboard.

What stories might go untold in the aftermath of our smashings and pinnings? What jokes demolished? What songs unsung?

Go in peace, little brown spider. You're welcome here.

Camphor (Cinnamomum camphora)

Stills the pain,
calms the skin,
unclogs the nostrils.

17

Isabelle limped from the bedroom cupping a spider in her hand. It was black and small and had been crawling across the top of the quilt when she woke up from her nap.

"What do you do with spiders around here?" she asked Grete, who had been discussing with Hen the finer points of collecting echinacea flowers from the roadside, both of them rocking in chairs on the front porch. Grete was knitting something on wooden needles, but Isabelle couldn't tell what. It didn't have sleeves. Could be a shawl, or maybe a parachute. Something interesting, Isabelle was positive. Grete didn't strike her as a knitter of the same old thing.

"We let them go on their way," Grete said. "That particular spider is named Travis. He is a traveler, an explorer, a news gatherer for his tribe."

"You know the name of each spider, miss?" Hen asked Grete, one eyebrow raised. "And what its job is?"

"Indeed I do, Hen. All you have to do is ask. Spiders are known to have loose lips. They can't seem to stop talking once they open their mouths."

"Didn't know they had lips at all, miss."

"A spider is a most complete creature." Grete laid down her knitting and stood up, reaching a hand toward Isabelle. "I'll put Travis back on his path. Isabelle, come have a seat. You shouldn't be moving about too much."

After Grete went inside, Hen pulled her chair closer to Isabelle's. "She's a strange one, don't you think?"

Isabelle considered this. She herself had been called strange all her life. "Strange" was the least of what she'd been called, but called it she was, almost every day. Even her own mother said to her from time to time, "Izzy, you're the strangest child," usually in response to a question Isabelle had asked, about ice cubes, for example, whether or not they ever felt cold to themselves, or something as simple as a pencil. "Do pencils have dreams?" she'd wondered out loud in first grade, staring somewhat dreamily herself at the No. 2 in her hand, ISABELLE BEENE inscribed in gold on its side (printer's error; happens all the time). "Where do you get such strange thoughts?" her mom asked in response. Isabelle didn't mind so much, her mom calling her strange, but she did wish she'd answer her questions.

Teachers whispered it in the hallway as Isabelle walked past, girls giggled it in the cafeteria as they watched Isabelle open her lunch box to reveal sandwiches made of hot dog buns and lavender jelly. Boys yelled it on the playground, along with "weirdo," "retard," and "doofus." Complete strangers called Isabelle strange.

But Isabelle never felt strange. She felt like herself.

She felt like an Isabelle Bean. What was so strange about that?

"No," Isabelle replied. "I don't think she's strange at all."

For dinner they ate a soup made out of ingredients neither of the girls quite recognized—twigs, it looked like, and some sort of tiny flowers in a broth that sighed a little sigh of woodland mushrooms—but it was good. They ate more salt bread and drank tea, though this tea was made from honeysuckle flowers and didn't make Isabelle sleepy.

It was a warm evening, and after dinner Isabelle, Hen, and Grete sat in the rockers on the front porch. Grete read to them from one of the books on her shelves, a story about a girl and boy who find a bird with a broken wing and bring it home. The story was filled with details about how one heals a bird (mashed marigolds, it turns out, and drops of clear springwater), and Isabelle didn't think she would get drawn in—she liked stories about magic and fairies more than ones about everyday children—but it wasn't long before she began cheering for the little bird's recovery (and wished the girl had been more on the ball—who would try to feed a bird moth wings to help it fly? Please!).

When the story was over, and Isabelle began to see what was around her again instead of the pictures the story had put in her mind, she found the porch was filled with birds—birds perched along the railing and the steps, birds sitting quietly at Grete's feet. Mourning doves, bluebirds, cardinals, sparrows, and three dozen brown wrens, all listening with the greatest attention.

Isabelle hugged her knees and pulled them to her chest. It had been more than an hour since they'd eaten, but she still felt surprisingly full.

And then she realized it wasn't so much that she felt full . . .

It was that she didn't feel lonely.

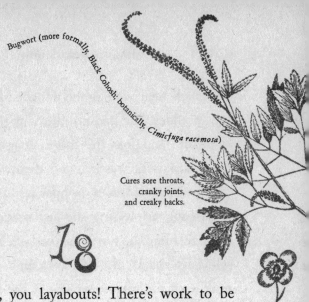

Bugwort (more formally, Black Cohosh; botanically, *Cimicfuga racemosa*)

Cures sore throats,
cranky joints,
and creaky backs.

18

"Up with ya, you layabouts! There's work to be done!"

Isabelle struggled to sit up. She wasn't sure where she was, only that her bed—bed? No, not a bed, but a cloud of blankets and quilts spread across the floor—was warm and entirely too comfortable to leave. Beside her, Hen sighed and rolled over. Isabelle nudged her.

"Five more minutes, Mam," Hen mumbled. "Jacob can milk the cow."

Isabelle giggled. "I'm not your mam," she said, poking Hen in the side with her finger.

Hen sat up on her elbows and squinted at Isabelle. "Oh, good morning, miss. Forgot where I was, I reckon."

Isabelle reached out and punched Hen lightly on the shoulder. She had no idea why she was feeling so punchy and poky this morning; usually when she felt this way she was irritated about something, but this morning it was the opposite—as if she found everything so pleasing she just needed to give it a squeeze. Here she was in her bed of clouds, the light piling up against the windows, in a cottage in the middle of the forest—or was it the middle of the woods? What was the difference? she wondered.

(The difference, she decided, had to do with what sort of story you were in—or in her case, what sort of story she had fallen into. You found forests in stories of enchantment and fantasy. Forests were homes to elves and fairies. Were humans even allowed in an enchanted forest? Good question. Isabelle would have to look it up later, but it seemed to her that forests were so magical that only the most special of humans—say, a changeling sort of a human—would be allowed in.

Woods, on the other hand, were earthier, populated by trolls and witches and woodsmen. Woods

crept up to the edges of villages and offered entice-
ments to their children. Spotted toadstools. Babbling
brooks. Could there be buried treasure in the woods?
No, Isabelle didn't think that sounded right. A wizard?
Probably not. A wicked queen in exile? Yes, Isabelle
decided. That was a distinct possibility.

As for changelings, well, they could show up
anywhere, woods or forest, city or suburb.
Changelings, to the best of Isabelle's knowledge,
were versatile and at home in a variety of settings.)

She leaned over and punched Hen again. "You
should stop calling me 'miss.' It's too fancy for"—
Isabelle had to push the word from her mouth, and
it came out more like a question—"friends?"

"Yes," Hen replied, yawning. "I suppose it is.
Are we friends then, miss? I mean, Isabelle?"

"Of course we are, Hen," Isabelle insisted, feeling
more sure of herself now. "We've been on a journey
together. That naturally makes us friends."

"Friends or no, you two lazy birds need to get out
of bed! I'm not running an inn here, now, am I?"
Grete stood over them, her hands on her hips. "'Tis

a business, and if you're going to stay here, you'd best do your part to keep it running."

So Hen scrambled out of bed and Isabelle almost scrambled out of bed, but remembered her ankle at the last second and sat back down to examine it. The swelling was gone but for a small bump. When Isabelle stood and put her weight on it, she felt the barest pinch of pain. So, not 100 percent healed; more like 96 percent. Isabelle shrugged. Close enough. She quickly dressed in the clothes Grete had laid out for her, a soft cotton shirt and a loose skirt.

"Come eat!" Grete called to the girls from the kitchen. "Then I'll put you to work."

Bowls of oatmeal sat steaming on the table alongside plates of thick toast spread with jam and butter. The girls ate quickly, then washed and dried their dishes, Isabelle dipping them into a soapy bucket of water, Hen drying with a flannel cloth.

"To the woods, then, for your first lesson." Grete stood in the doorway with a basket in her hand. "You're not scared of critters or creepy and crawly things, are ya? The woods here are wild woods."

Hen laughed, as though the very idea of her being afraid of insects or animals was too preposterous to take seriously. "Only things that scare me are inside a house—clothes that need mending, babes that need bathing." She turned to Isabelle. "Anything outside a house scare you?"

Isabelle shook her head no, but it was not the most convincing shake of the head ever shook in this world. Spiders, she could handle. Squirrels, not a problem. Snakes?

The little hairs on her arms stood at attention. Please, she thought, don't let there be snakes in these woods.

"For the kind of work I do, you've got to use your eyes and your nose, and sometimes you've got to use your teeth and tongue as well," Grete said, crouching beside a patch of unruly-looking weeds twenty yards past the cottage gate. Well, they looked like weeds to Isabelle. But the way Grete was so careful to pluck one of the plants by its roots and hold it almost lovingly up for Isabelle and Hen to examine made her think perhaps one girl's weeds were another woman's roses.

"Rattle root," Grete told them. "Listen."

She shook the plant's stalk, and the seed pods growing from its branches made a light, rattling noise. "For rheumatism and women's problems," Grete explained, standing. "You steep it in alcohol and water for fourteen days, shaking it every day, to make a tincture. A dose is maybe five or ten drops, no more than thirty drops a day."

Grete took a few more steps, then reached down again to pull up another plant. "Snakeroot. You dry the roots, then pound them into a powder. It'll cure an earache or a toothache in no time, but if too much is taken, it'll make you ill."

And so the lessons continued for the rest of the morning. Isabelle liked the names of the plants—bugwort, richweed, squawroot, dog rose—but quickly scrambled the various uses and doses and preparations. Did you dry pennyroyal or boil it? Prescribe drops of feverfew or brews? She didn't much care, and after a while stopped paying attention.

"Are you hearing anything I'm saying, Isabelle?" Grete demanded after giving a lengthy lecture on something called a whig plant.

"My brain is full," Isabelle told her. "It's too stuffed to take in one more fact."

Grete sighed. "You too, Hen?"

But Hen shook her head. "I think it's fascinating, miss."

"Well, I suppose it's time for lunch, by the look of the sky," Grete said, picking up her basket, now full of roots and stems and leaves and berries. "Hen, this afternoon we can work in the kitchen. I'll show you how to go about drying the roots and leaves, and how to boil syrups. Isabelle—" Grete stared at Isabelle quizzically, as though she couldn't think of one single thing for Isabelle to do. "Perhaps— perhaps this afternoon you should rest. There'll be work you can help with later."

Isabelle almost protested that she could help too, that her ankle was fine—she'd been on it all morning, hadn't she?—and then decided against it. She could see herself on the front porch reading a book, rocking back and forth, maybe eating something chocolate. Did Grete have chocolate?

"There are some small cakes, if that's what you're thinking," Grete said, and Isabelle took a step back. Yes, that was what she'd been thinking. But how could Grete know?

Grete had to shake Isabelle awake when she finally had work for her to do later that afternoon. Isabelle wiped a bit of drool from the corner of her mouth and rubbed her eyes. She'd been reading one of Grete's books. To her surprise, when she'd stood in front of the bookshelves and began pulling books, she found they were all handwritten, each one in the same slippery blue cursive, the kind that looked pretty but turned out to be hard to decipher. So Grete was an author, Isabelle had thought, and grabbed several books at random to take with her to the porch.

The story she'd been reading was about a girl who wandered along a wooded path and made friends with all sorts of things—bluebirds, squirrels, butterflies, trees. Everything she met had a secret to tell. After a while, carrying all the different secrets made her sleepy, and just as the girl lay down beneath a butterfly bush to take a nap, Isabelle had felt her eyes grow heavy too.

Grete picked up the book from Isabelle's lap. "Do you know it's impossible to finish this book? I fell asleep three or four times while writing it, and I've never been able to read through it since the moment I jotted the last period."

"Is it magic?" Isabelle asked, suddenly feeling more awake. "Maybe the book casts a spell on the person reading it."

Grete looked away for a moment. "Couldn't say." Waving Isabelle toward the kitchen, she ordered, "Come along inside. Hen and I've been hard at work, and now here's the part where you can help."

In the kitchen, Grete pointed to a wide array of pots and jars on the counter. "As you can see, we have syrups and tinctures and powders and leaves.

Hen and I have boiled and chopped and sorted and pounded, and now it is time to package things up and put them on the porch. Tonight, while we're asleep, the folks will come, and in the morning there'll be the fun of seeing what's been left. The last of the fall's apples and potatoes? A few jars of honey? A paper packet of sugar? If there's sugar and honey, I'll make Isabelle more sweets."

"So they pay you for your medicine?" Hen asked, running a damp rag across the kitchen table.

"Meager pay it is, too, most of it, but it's what folks can pay with, and money won't help me out here in the woods, will it?"

"How do you know they need the medicine?"

Grete picked up a tangled strand of twine from the counter and began working at the knots. "Notes, mostly. Some send their little ones with a message— 'the baby has a fever' and the like. If they have questions, they get word to me. They send an older boy or someone full grown to pick up their packages at night, so as not to get on the wrong side of the village apothecary or the priest. A woman in the woods is always suspicious to them that are in charge."

"I ain't met an apothecary worth his salt yet," Hen said, washing her hands at the sink. "Ours is always giving Mam potions that don't help a lick. You can do more with a cool cloth and a bit of vinegar than the apothecary can do with his whole store of roots and powders."

"Perhaps you'll apprentice to a healer when you're older," Grete suggested. "I'd say you have the gift for it."

Hen reddened, then seemed suddenly fascinated with a speck on her shoe. "Be nice to have a gift for something," she said after a moment. "But they don't let girls apprentice, now, do they?"

Grete harrumphed. "A bunch of fools, the lot who came up with that system. You lose half the world's brainpower that way."

"It is the way it is, I guess," Hen replied with a shrug. She picked up a small sack of something and handed it to Isabelle. "This here's boneset, for them what's got the fever. I'll show you what Grete's taught me so far about measuring and pouring out. Nothing hard about it in the least."

To her surprise, Isabelle found she enjoyed scooping powders onto squares of brown paper and folding the paper into neat triangles. She liked using a dropper to drip liquids into tiny blue bottles, and found it satisfying to pour the red and purple syrups into jars. She enjoyed it even though Grete hovered over her, counting out drops as they dripped and making her remeasure her scoops.

"Why aren't you watching Hen?" Isabelle asked. Grete's breath on the back of her neck as she shadowed Isabelle's every move was beginning to annoy her. "Hen might make a mistake, you never know."

"Hen won't make a mistake. Hen's careful."

Hen looked up from the table, where she was grinding leaves into a powder, her eyes wide, as though surprised to hear such a thing said about her.

"If Hen's careful, then what am I?" Isabelle asked.

Grete laughed. "You, Isabelle, are a dreamer. You

always have to keep an eye on the dreamers. My husband was one, now, wasn't he?"

Isabelle turned around and looked at her. "Your husband? You're married?"

"Was. I'm a widow, going on fifty years now," Grete said. "One marriage was enough for me."

"I won't ever get married," said Hen. "Don't want to get weighed down with babies."

"A baby's not a bad thing," Grete said. "You might find you want one later."

"Maybe." Hen sounded doubtful. "But Mam's got five little ones other than me, and it's brought me no end of troubles. I'm supposed to take care of 'em, being the oldest, but I'm always losing this one or that one, or getting the brush caught in the other one's hair. Seems I can make a baby cry faster than any girl in the village."

"You've got other talents," Grete told her. "How about you, Isabelle?" Grete once again peered over Isabelle's shoulder as Isabelle poured syrup into a jar. "Do you want a man and a baby someday?"

Isabelle shrugged. "I can't imagine liking someone enough to marry him."

"Do you know no nice boys?"

Isabelle pondered this for the briefest of moments.
"No," she said, shaking her head. She didn't mention that up until Hen, she hadn't known many nice
girls, either.

Grete patted Isabelle on the back. "One will
come along. You've had hard times, to be sure, but
things will get easier for you. You'll see."

Isabelle wondered if Grete could tell she'd had
hard times just by looking at her. She supposed it
was possible. But her deep-down feeling? Grete
could see inside of people, into their hearts and
minds.

In fact, Isabelle felt that surely Grete was magic.

But what kind of magic did Grete possess?

Ah, a question that deserved an answer if ever
one did.

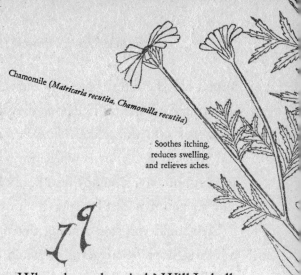

Chamomile (*Matricaria recutita, Chamomilla recutita*)

Soothes itching,
reduces swelling,
and relieves aches.

I know, I know. What about the witch? Will Isabelle find the witch? Is she still looking for the witch? Or has Isabelle's search come to an end? But if it has, then what? Do we leave Isabelle and Hen happily ever after in the woods with Grete, picking berries? Do they grow up there, tending to Grete in her old age, taking over her "business" when she passes into the Great Unknown?

That could be a good story, don't you think? Lacking in excitement, admittedly. Perhaps more the thing your grandmother would read with her First Monday of the Month book group. Remember that time you had to go with her? How the hostess's house smelled like a hundred cats lived there, but it turned out she didn't have any cats at all, just one shivering Chihuahua? The book they discussed that night was something like *A Rosebush for Rosemary*, and you vowed that even when you were old as the ancient hills, you wouldn't read books like that. No, only adventure books for you.

So, should you stop reading this book? I mean, you thought you were getting a witch, and so far all you've gotten is two girls and an old woman herb doctor. I don't blame you for wanting your money back. You saved your receipt, right? Let's march right back to the bookstore and demand—

Wait a minute.

I thought I saw something.

Yes, I'm pretty sure I saw something over— over—over—

There.

It's a piece of paper falling out of a book.

I wonder what it says.

20

A few days later, when Isabelle was on the porch reading, a piece of paper slipped out of the book and fell to the floor.

It was a folded sheet of thick drawing paper, yellowing around the edges, crumbling at the corners. Isabelle leaned down and picked it up. Read: *For Isabelle*. She carefully unfolded it to reveal a nighttime picture drawn in blue-black ink—stars along the top, a full moon, a clearing in the woods, a patch of grass lit by the moon's pale light. The trees that stood around the clearing had a friendly look to Isabelle, as though they were glad it was finally spring. Something was strung between the two trees in the foreground—

was it a blanket? No, Isabelle thought, a hammock.

A hammock. And in the hammock—Isabelle didn't even have to look. She did look, though, and so she saw the baby, round and glowing, so small. She could tell the baby wasn't at all scared to be outside in the middle of the night. She could tell just by looking—just by feeling the feelings the picture made her feel as she looked at it.

But as she sat gazing at the picture, another feeling gathered at the edges of the paper where her fingers grasped it. Fear. The trees had felt it first. The trees had heard the children coming through the woods. They'd heard the whispering voices, the hands reaching down to the ground to scoop up rocks and stones. The trees knew who was coming—

21

—and they knew what the children would do next.

22

Isabelle was still sitting in the chair, the book still on her lap, when Grete came out from the kitchen to the porch. Did Grete look different to Isabelle now? Isabelle squinted her eyes, opened them wide, tilted her head left, then right, as she watched Grete walk out to the front yard to check on a patch of silverweed she was cultivating by the woodpile. Does someone's face look meaner when you've discovered their darkest secret? Sadder? The lines around their eyes and the corners of their mouth deeper now, more full of grief, rage, terror, horror?

Even at a distance, Grete looked like Grete, older than Isabelle's mother, younger than the old ladies she saw riding to the store on the bus, their hands folded carefully atop their purses. Her eyes still looked kind, the skin of her cheeks still looked downy and soft. She didn't appear the least bit like a—well, Isabelle could barely bring herself to think it.

Isabelle looked up to the tops of the trees. She looked for the bones of children dangling from the branches, but saw none. She felt foolish.

And then Isabelle looked at the picture she held in her hands. The trees no longer appeared happy, the moon no longer glowed.

The hammock was empty.

"I see you've been reading," Grete said, remounting the steps to the porch. "Those stories of mine probably aren't as exciting as the stories you're used to, but you might learn something, you never know."

"You don't ever know," Isabelle agreed, shutting the book. She reached into her lap to slip the picture back between the book's pages—

But the picture was gone.

Grete leaned her face next to Isabelle's and whispered, "Don't be afraid. But don't say anything to

Hen. She's a good girl, but she's lived in fear a long time, and there's no telling what she'll do if she finds out."

Isabelle nodded.

"We've things to talk about, you and I," Grete said, and headed inside just as Hen came bounding into the yard, waving a bundle of leaves at Isabelle. "Goldenseal! It heals everything!"

Hen went on for a few minutes about the miraculous properties of goldenseal, and while she did, Isabelle's mind raced over possibilities and probabilities and practicalities. Grete, in her way, had just told Isabelle, *Yes, I am.* She had just told Isabelle, *Don't tell.* Was that a threat? It hadn't sounded like a threat, but now Isabelle wondered.

She looked at Hen. Would Hen even believe her? Well, Hen *did* believe there was a witch, Isabelle reasoned, so it wouldn't be like trying to make someone like Charley Bender believe. Charley Bender—who for all Isabelle knew was still standing at the door of the nurse's office, waiting for Isabelle to pop back up—probably pooh-poohed the very idea of witches, but Hen's whole life had been lived in the shadow of one.

Hen. At dinner the night before, a savory pumpkin pie seasoned with acorn shavings and lilyweed, she'd reminisced about the pumpkin soup her mother made on cold winter days. It was Hen who was sent to the root cellar to select two or three of the small, round pumpkins they'd stored there after the autumn harvest, because Hen knew from a look which pumpkins were best for soup and which were best for throwing out to the pigs.

"You knew Mam had a mind set on pumpkin soup when she told Jacob to skim the cream off the top of the milk and bring it into the kitchen first thing instead of taking it to market to sell of a morning," Hen told them, spooning a bite of pie into her mouth. "Cream and a dash of nutmeg is what gives Mam's soup its flavor. Of course, there's hours of stewing and stirring to be done first, to get the pumpkin meat soft as it can be. Sugar, she's the one you give the spoon to. Four years old, but right sensible. Not like Artemis, who's six but without a straight thought in his head. That one's topsy-turvy."

Hen had four brothers and one sister: Jacob, Callou, Artemis, Sugar, and Pip. Hen was in charge of the whole brigade, as her mother was always busy cooking and baking and laundering and fixing and patching and cooking and cooking and cooking. Her father was rarely home. "Da is a peddler on the road, selling his wares across the Five Villages and beyond. He's home in the coldest of the winter months, but rarely elsewise. Ah, but it's lovely when he's there. He reads us stories and tells us tales and lets us lie in bed of a morning while he milks the cows."

"I'd think it be nice to have such a large family," Grete commented as she poured herself some more tea. "Someone to play with at all hours of the day."

"It's not my job to play with 'em, it's my job to mind 'em, and I'd do a better job of it if there were only one or two," Hen said with a sigh. "I wish I was the youngest and not the oldest. If I were youngest, then I could run about and play Wallop the Dragon with all the rest. Instead I'm chasing the little ones around in circles, and I'm no good at it. I try to be good at it, I do. But they're always running away from me."

"Where are all those brothers and sisters of yours now?" Grete asked. "Back home?"

Hen picked worriedly at a hangnail. "Off at the camps outside of Greenan, I suppose. They got away from me when we were heading up that way, and then I took up with this one." She nodded toward Isabelle. "I guess I let them get away on purpose. Thought it might be fun to have an adventure on my own."

If Hen was worried about her brothers and sisters, she didn't say. Would she be more worried or less, Isabelle wondered now, if she found out the witch was ten feet away from where she sat? Maybe it was best not to find out. Remembering Hen's desire to wrap her hands around the witch's neck when she set sights on her, Isabelle shivered. Who knew what Hen would do?

And who knew what Grete had planned for them?

Maybe, Isabelle thought, it was time for a change of venue. For everyone's sake.

"Hen," she said in a quiet voice, sure that Grete couldn't hear them from the kitchen. "Do you think we should be going soon?"

Hen, who had not finished reporting on the joys of goldenseal, stopped short. "But why? Grete is happy to have us, and there's no place else for me to go. I'd wonder if there were any place else for you to go either."

Hen had a point. Where would Isabelle wander off to if she left? She had already reached her destination, hadn't she? She'd set out to find the witch, and apparently she'd found her. A disappointment of a witch, to be honest, not the least bit scary, no evil fumes steaming off her skin, a house filled with sunlight and healing plants, but a witch nonetheless.

"Well, sooner or later, we'll have to go, won't we?" Isabelle asked.

"Surely," Hen replied. "But not during the season. We've come to a safe place, and we might as well stay until we wear out our welcome."

But was this a safe place? Isabelle wondered. Was it safe for Hen, safe for Grete? For the rest of the day she peeked around corners, slinked through the yard, looked up and down and all around, watching and waiting for something to—to what? Jump out at her? Catch her in a trap? Reveal itself? *Oh, here we are, a pile of bones, just as you've been told.*

That night after dinner, when it was time to sit on the porch and read, Grete pulled a thin volume from the bookshelf and blew the dust from its cover. She sat in the middle rocking chair, and Hen and Isabelle sat on either side of her, Hen happily, Isabelle warily.

"Once upon a time," Grete began, "there was a woman who lived in the woods with her husband and child, and they were very happy."

Comfrey (Symphytum officinale)

Knits broken bones back together, fights infection.

23

But then the husband died.

The wife did what she could to make a life for herself and her baby. She hunted the woods for mushrooms and roots and healing plants, anything she could sell to the villagers to survive. The villagers bought the woman's goods, but did not welcome her into their homes. She and her husband had moved to the woods from another place, and so were strangers, and unwelcome. After her husband's death, the woman was no more welcome than she had been before, though from time to time a good-hearted villager left her a basket of potatoes or apples on her back porch, a loaf or two of bread, so she and the child wouldn't starve.

How did the stories start? A woman alone in the woods, I suppose, is always suspicious. So it was no surprise that the village children spied on her and told tales about the baby, that horns grew out of the baby's forehead, that she had a forked tongue.

The woman had always possessed certain gifts. From the time she was small she knew people's names without being told, could peer into their minds, see their stories. She had the healing touch, could make words and pictures dance on the page. As a child, her family had moved many times, to keep her safe. Once her gifts were discovered, people tended to start terrible rumors about her, call her names, whisper how it would be better if she were burned at the stake, send the devil running. But because she heard the whispers in her sleep, her family always escaped in time.

The night her life changed forever, she'd heard the whispers in the trees, but the moon was full, its light bright, which confused the leaves and tangled the words and made them impossible to understand. What were the trees saying? She didn't know, so she went about her evening chores with a heavy feeling and not a thing she could do about it.

When a rock hit the side of the house, she ran into the yard and found the baby already abloom in bruises, a trickle of blood staining her forehead. The woman ran with the baby into the house, then ran out again, a jagged rock in her hand, but no one was there.

And when she went back inside, the baby was gone as well.

24

"So did you ever kill anyone?" Isabelle asked later, when Hen had gone inside to bed.

"Only one," Grete replied.

"That's an awful story!" Hen cried, thinking Grete was finished. "She found the baby again, didn't she?"

Grete shook her head. "The baby was gone for good, I'm afraid. Listen to what the story says." She held up the book. "'And the woman knew the fairies had taken the baby for a changeling, and that the baby would be sent to another world, and would, most likely, not return.'"

Hen reddened. "A changeling! Only a newborn can be a changeling! Besides, if the baby had been taken for a changeling, what did the fairies leave in exchange?"

"A note, it says here," Grete replied, running her

finger down the page. "'No baby will ever be safe in these woods,' the note read, 'and so we shall not leave another in this one's place.'"

"This story should be tossed onto the rubbish heap!" Hen stood, looked indignant, held out her hand. "I'll do the job myself, if you'd like."

Grete handed her the book. "Yes, I suppose you're right," she said with a sigh. "It's a story that doesn't bear retelling."

Isabelle stared at her. Grete couldn't mean that, of course. She was just placating Hen. How could this story—Grete's story, for Isabelle knew the story belonged to Grete—not be told ever again, especially—

26

"I heard a child laughing in the woods outside the house the next day," Grete explained to Isabelle. "And my thoughts brought a heavy branch down on his head."

27

—especially since Isabelle had decided it was her story too.

28

I often think about people who get what they think they wanted. Lottery winners. Child movie stars. Everyone has some sort of wish, a dream, that they know won't come true. Except that one time in a million it does.

But it seems like every few months the newspaper carries a story about the lottery winner who complains that money has ruined his life. Or about the young actress who has everything except happiness.

What is it about dreams coming true? Is it because we want the wrong things? Is it because no dream ever really comes true, at least not in the way we envisioned it coming true? The lottery winner finds that money indeed can't buy everything, particularly love, and the celebrity learns that having people looking at you all the time and trying to touch you and generally wanting to eat you up like a tuna fish sandwich, well, it's not all that it's cracked up to be.

And what of the changeling? You've known you were one all your life. You've felt it. I'm talking to you, lying there on the bed eating Twizzlers and collecting cavities—and you, over there, reading this while you should be doing your math homework. I know you know that I know you know what I mean. And what you think is this: If only you could go back to your real home, to your real family, everything would fall into place and you would be loved and admired all hours of the day and you'd get to eat as much chocolate as you'd like without feeling sick or having the tiniest pimple pop up on your chin.

But real life is real life, isn't it? Which is to say, it's not perfect, even when things go your way. Of course, most days things don't go our way, we don't win the big prize, the cute boy or girl doesn't smile at us, our teachers don't suddenly discover our true and hidden genius. We're used to minor defeats. We expect them. But we also expect that when our dreams finally do come true, it will be like the movies—our whole lives perfect and aglow, forever and ever, amen.

What do I know about it? you wonder. What makes me such a big expert? Am I speaking from experience?

As a matter of fact, I am.

29

Isabelle and Grete were quiet for a long time after Hen went to bed. Finally Isabelle said, "Do you want me to go dig the book out of the trash?"

"No need," Grete replied. "It's rewriting itself as we speak. Go stand next to the shelf by the south window and you'll hear the scribbling. I've tried throwing that story away many a time. I even burned it once. And then I'd go to the shelf to pull out what I thought was a book on birds or rose-bushes, but it turned out to be the story again. If I didn't read it, it filled all the other books on the shelves. So I read it when it appears, and it lets me be for a while."

Isabelle peered across the yard. Her eyes came to

rest on a flowering bush, forsythia maybe, yellow, cheerful buds popping out from its branches, so bright she could see them even in the fading light. She tried to think about a story rewriting itself. Were the words the same every time? Or were there small changes with each new version— the baby wrapped in a pale yellow blanket in one story, and in a lavender one the next time the story was read? Was the baby sometimes a boy, sometimes a girl? Was the baby always Isabelle?

Grete stood up and leaned slightly over the porch railing, as though to smell the pink roses climbing up the latticework. "I lived outside of Greenan when they took the baby—"

Isabelle sat forward in her seat. "The fairies, you mean?"

"I always supposed it was." Grete looked at Isabelle, her expression somewhere between a grimace and a grin. "Funny thing is, I never believed in fairies. Still don't know if I do. But how else could the baby have crossed over?"

"Crossed over where?"

"The other world. Your world."

Isabelle took a deep breath. "Oh, I see. I mean, because it would have had to cross over, right? If it was me, that is. The baby."

Looking startled, Grete took a step back. "You? Oh, dear—you think that baby was you?"

"Well, yes, I mean, that's why I'm here, isn't it?" Suddenly Isabelle didn't feel quite so sure. "Because I'm a changeling? On my way back to my true home? Which is this house?"

"You? A changeling? Child, the notions that fill your head!" Grete sat down heavily on a chair, the laughter rumbling out of her. "You're no more a changeling than I'm an ostrich."

Isabelle stared down at the porch's broad planks. Her red boots, she noticed, had grown scratched and scuffed after days of wandering through the woods. Her brain felt scratched and scuffed too. Not a changeling? Not the baby in the hammock? Tears formed in the corners of her eyes, but she furiously blinked them away. She'd been so sure! Wasn't that why the picture had fallen out of the book into her hands? That was what Grete had intended to happen, wasn't it? So Isabelle would know that Grete was her real mother, that her mother on the other side, in the other world, wherever it was that Isabelle had come from, had just been a substitute mother until Isabelle could find her way to her real home.

Her mother. Isabelle had hardly thought about her mother—her "mother"—in the days she'd been at Grete's, and suddenly she could see her pacing up and down the linoleum of their long, narrow kitchen, tugging at the handkerchief she kept anchored beneath her wristwatch, stopping to listen at the window, as though she might hear Isabelle's voice outside in the yard.

"Yes, girl, you're seeing it now." Grete's voice broke into her thoughts. "Your mother was the baby. Your mother was the one stolen away."

"My mother is the changeling?" Isabelle's mouth dropped open. Her *mother*?

Grete walked across the porch and sat down in the rocker next to Isabelle. "Think about it, child. If my babe was stolen near fifty years ago, do you think it could be you? You're—what? Eleven? Twelve? Not even close to going on fifty."

"Maybe time doesn't work the same way in every world," Isabelle offered lamely.

"Time is time. You can't change it. Oh, a minute here or there, for sure. You can swallow up a week or two if need be. But years? No."

Isabelle started to offer another argument about how time might shift itself around, but stopped herself. Repeated herself: "My mother is the changeling?"

Grete nodded, and Isabelle rocked back in her chair as far as she could, her head hanging back so that the world appeared upside down to her eyes. "So that makes me a half changeling, right?" she asked in an upside-down-sounding voice.

"I suppose it does," Grete answered. "If such a thing can be said to exist."

Isabelle sat straight up, and her brains twirled around in her head. Her stomach felt loopy, the way it did on the first downward slope of the roller coaster at Fun World. "Is my mother magic? Am I half-magic?"

"Not much magic in this family, I'm afraid," Grete said with a shrug. "Healing powers, for sure, and thought reading. Nothing fancy. But I suppose what little of it there is, your mother has it. Don't know if it got passed on to you or not."

Isabelle ransacked her memory for evidence that her mother could read minds or mend broken bones. But all she came up with were images of a normal, middle-aged woman doing normal, middle-aged things, getting ready for work, chopping an onion while a pat of butter sputtered in the pan on the stove beside her, picking bits of lint off Isabelle's navy blue sweater.

"Maybe you have to know that you're magic to practice magic," Isabelle said, feeling let down.

"It's possible," Grete replied. She paused for a moment, then said, "So, tell me about her. What is she like? Does she look like me?"

Isabelle peered at her grandmother—her grandmother!—through the dim light. Grete looked eager, like a little kid asking about what she might get for Christmas this year. "She has blue eyes like you do. But her nose is—pudgier, I guess."

Grete nodded. "That would be my husband's nose. Your mother had it even as a baby."

"She's nice," Isabelle continued. "She doesn't yell too much. She, uh . . ."

Grete leaned forward. "Yes?"

Isabelle shrugged. "She's a mom. She goes to work, she comes home to make dinner. On Saturday she goes grocery shopping."

"Yes, I suppose she would," Grete said, sounding disappointed. "Oh, I do wish I could see her for myself. I can track her whereabouts and get a general idea of things. But to actually be able to see her!"

"She got As in math in school," Isabelle said, relieved to have one more bit of information to report. "And she looks pretty when she smiles."

Grete smiled, and Isabelle could see her mother in the old woman's face. Her mother, the changeling. That night, as Isabelle lay in bed, she twisted her imagination this way and that, trying to see her mother as a magical being, a person who had been taken by fairies as a baby. Her mother had been stolen by fairies! It was almost impossible to believe, but Isabelle tried as hard as she could. After all, didn't this news change everything? Once Isabelle told her mother she was magic, who knew what sort of things the two of them—the magic mother and the half-magic daughter—might make happen.

Which raised a question for Isabelle. No, make that two questions.

How on earth would she ever get home?

And just what was she doing here in the first place?

30

When Isabelle walked into the kitchen the next morning, her eyes still cloudy with sleep, she found a knapsack leaning against the wall beside the back door. Grete stood at the stove, stirring something in a pot.

"So you'll be off today, then," Grete said, not turning around. She sounded as though she were continuing a conversation instead of starting one. "To the camps north of Greenan."

"I will?" Isabelle asked. She rubbed her eyes. Had she missed something? "Are you kicking me out?"

Grete glanced at Isabelle over her shoulder. "Putting you to work, is more like it. Now that I've brought you down here, there's something I need you to do."

Isabelle stumbled against a chair, then lowered herself into it. "What do you mean, you brought me down here?"

"Exactly that. I got you to open the door, which wasn't difficult at all. You were ready." Grete put a lid on the pan and set the spoon on a cloth by the stove. "I tried for years to get your mother to come, but I never could, even when she was young."

Isabelle puzzled over this. "Why not? She was in an orphanage. Why wouldn't she want to come home?"

"Because she didn't know she had a home. And there was the problem of the imagination." Grete turned toward Isabelle and tapped her head. "The ability to see things that aren't there and to hope that what you see could be real. You have to be able to put your hand on a doorknob and believe that something completely unexpected lies beyond the door. Your mother never had that kind of imagination."

Grete began brushing little sprigs of leaves and twigs from the counter into her hand. "It took years to find her in the first place. Had to let my mind wander to the places in the other world I thought she might be. I could feel her, you see; and after a while, I could track her thoughts. They'd come to me in little bursts of words. Baby words at first— 'Fire hot!' 'Dog bite!'—but then more complicated thinking. One day, when she was about nine, the matron at the orphanage had her memorize her address. So then I knew exactly where she was. But it turned out to be useless information. Your mother was scared of the dark. She was scared of other children. I could know her thoughts, but I couldn't intrude on them to explain things to her."

She tossed the bits and pieces she'd gathered into the sink and wiped her hands on her apron. "In short, your mother was not the kind of girl who would open a door and hope she would fall into another world. So I could never get her to one of the doors."

Isabelle blinked. Blinked again. "There's more than one door?"

"What do you think, girl? There's doors all over

creation. And the children who want to find them find them, and the children who don't want to, don't. Your mother didn't want to find one—"

"But I did," Isabelle finished for her.

"I knew it from the minute you were born."

Isabelle walked over to the counter and tore a hunk of bread from the loaf on the cutting board. "So you got me instead of my mother, and now you're sending me away."

Grete stepped closer to Isabelle, as though she meant to share a secret. "I want you to go to the camps and tell the children my story. Make them see I'm not a witch—that there's no witch at all."

"Who's not a witch?" Hen stood at the door, a bundle of dried roots in her arms, her eyes wide. "What do you mean you're not a witch? Who said you were a witch?"

"Hen," Grete said in an even voice. "I thought you were outside."

"What do you mean you're not a witch?" Hen repeated in a trembling voice.

Isabelle felt confused. "Wait a second. I thought

you *were* a witch. Not a bad witch or anything, but a witch."

Grete gave Isabelle a sharp look. "Now don't go talking like that. I'm not a witch. I've got powers. I don't use them for bad; half the time they come unbidden. One of the few times I've done anything on purpose—"

"What? When?" Isabelle asked eagerly.

"Was to get you here. I've been waiting many a year for you to be old enough to help."

Hen's eyes sparked. "If there's not a witch that kills little ones, then who's killing them?"

"Nobody!" Grete shook her head in disgust. "Not one child has been killed!" She paused. Revised. "Only one child has been killed."

(And here's when she told Isabelle and Hen the story: the boy in the woods the day after the baby disappeared, Grete's powers unleashed as if by their own volition, the branch falling, falling, Grete yelling for the boy to move, the boy standing there frozen and then toppling with the weight of the branch as it hit him, and then still as a stone.)

Grete faced both girls. "If I'd come forward, if I'd walked out of the woods with that boy's body in my arms, I would have been put to death on the spot. So I ran. Ran for years until I finally settled here, where nobody knew me, where nobody had ever seen my face before."

"So the people around here, they don't have any idea?" Isabelle asked. "I mean, who you are?"

"They know that I'm Grete the Healer," Grete replied. She sighed. "But I suppose that's not what you mean. Do they know I'm the witch? The so-called witch? Of course not. I'd be dead in the ground if they did."

Isabelle grabbed Grete's wrist. "You have to tell them! Otherwise it will go on forever!"

"What do you think I'm talking about, girl?" Grete looked as though she didn't know whether to laugh or cry. "I know it must be told. And now you're here to do the telling. You're the only one I can trust to get the job done, child of my child that you are. If you don't, you're right—it will go on forever. I'll be dead and gone, and they'll go on believing that there's a witch in the woods eating their babies. The stories get worse with every generation."

Isabelle took a deep breath. If she could put an end to the fear and the running just by standing up and telling the truth, she supposed she ought—

"I think you ought to be strung from the highest tree."

Hen stood in the middle of the kitchen, still clutching her bundle of roots. "You've had a good life all these years, making your potions and brews, while the rest of us have been running off into the woods, thinking death was riding on our tails. It's a horrible thing you've done, not coming forward."

Grete stared stonily into the air for a few moments before she replied. "I hoped that by being a healer, I could make up for some of it. Hoped I could even things out. Because"—and here she turned toward Hen, looked her in the eye—"I wasn't willing to die. Not for a minute, not for something that happened by accident. Do you blame me, Hen?"

Hen threw the dried plants to the floor, where

they disintegrated into pieces and crumbs. "I don't blame you," she snarled, barreling past Isabelle toward the back door. "But I won't ever forgive you either."

The door slammed behind her. Grete sat down at the table, looked up at Isabelle. "You'll do it, won't you, Isabelle? Tell the other children?"

Isabelle swallowed hard. She nodded. "I should go talk to Hen first, though."

"Go," Grete told her, rubbing her face with her hands. "Go see about Hen." She looked up at Isabelle, her eyes rimmed in red. She opened her mouth as if she had more to say, but the only thing she said was, "Go. Now."

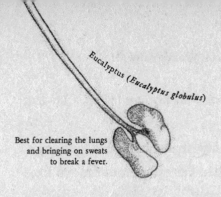

Eucalyptus (*Eucalyptus globulus*)

Best for clearing the lungs and bringing on sweats to break a fever.

31

How many hours had Hen trailed Isabelle on the path north? How many hours had Hen been muttering and mumbling about the kind of trouble she was going to be in, the way she'd let the children run off on their own, what could she have been thinking about, wasn't Mam going to boil over when she found out, and for what? For *what*? Hen kept asking the trees and the birds and the air. So that Hen could help a killer make her potions?

"She's not a killer," Isabelle chirped in a singsong voice from time to time. "She's a healer."

"'*She's a healer,*'" Hen mocked back. "Oh, is she? Seems to me she admitted to at least one killing. I'd wager there are more she's not confessed. Old liar, that one is."

Isabelle could only shake her head and sigh. Occasionally she rolled her eyes. From time to time she tried to put herself in Hen's shoes. She'd be angry too, wouldn't she? After years and years of being terrified, sent running from home whenever the wind blew in a rumor of a witch nearby? *What kind of nightmares these kids must have,* Isabelle thought. Witchy, baby-eating nightmares. She shuddered.

On the other hand, Hen *was* talking about Isabelle's grandmother, which Isabelle was pretty sure violated a bunch of etiquette rules. Besides, Isabelle was just now getting to enjoy the idea of having a grandmother, and quite frankly, Hen was spoiling things.

"You don't have to follow me," Isabelle told Hen around hour three of their trek. "There's probably another path you could go on, a shortcut through the woods or something."

"I know all about your shortcuts," Hen sputtered.

"Shortcut to a troll's bridge, most likely. Or an ogre's den. No, I'll keep to this path, if it's all the same."

"Fine," Isabelle said. "Whatever."

There were all sorts of things Isabelle was eager to think about, if only Hen wasn't behind her grumbling. Her mother, for one. Just wait until Isabelle told her! She figured her mom would need to be trained how to use whatever gifts she had. What if Isabelle could help her communicate telepathically with Grete? Then the two of them could have mother-daughter conversations in their minds, and maybe Isabelle could join in. Isabelle was determined to develop whatever magical powers she had. She had to have some, right? She and her mom could check out some books from the library, start doing research online, learn how to put their magic to use—

"Old spotty-faced cow," Hen muttered.

—do some sort of exercises for increasing their mind-reading abilities. And Isabelle would really like to dig deeper into how to make books write and rewrite themselves. She thought this might have some practical applications when it came to writing essays for school. You could start out with an essay on, say, "The Person Who Has Affected Me the Most in My Life," and it might morph into "What I Want to Do to Change the World," and then "World Peace: Is It Possible?" Isabelle thought if she figured out the trick, she might only have to write one essay for the rest of her education career—

"Wart-nosed, one-eyed toad," Hen continued.

—not that Isabelle hated to write, she just wished her teachers would come up with better topics. Although she had to admit, if she was ever asked to write an essay on "Grandparents, Why They Matter," she'd have a ton to say. But who would believe her? Well, as long as her mom believed—

"Ring-butted, red-eared, snip-snouted hyena," Hen added.

But Isabelle was getting ahead of herself. First, the kids in the camps. Safe to assume they'd respond exactly the same way Hen had? Isabelle supposed so. But as long as they believed Isabelle, that was all that mattered. They could go home, stay home, grow up, raise families. Sooner or later they'd forget all about Grete—

"Ought to chase the dirty worm-eater with sticks and rocks."

—or maybe they wouldn't. If Hen, who had admired Grete and had certainly at one time had fond feelings for her, was back there snorting and bleating about beating Grete with sticks and rocks, then Isabelle might have a real problem on her hands. What if the kids at the camp wanted to do worse to Grete than just throw rocks at her?

Isabelle felt in her pocket. Before they'd left, Grete had taken her aside and handed her a small pouch. "If you get in a bad spot, this can help. You just sprinkle it on the ground. It calms folks, soothes their feelings."

Isabelle looked at Grete, tilted her head to one side. "Is this a potion? I thought you said you weren't a witch."

"It's not a potion, and I'm not a witch." Grete sounded as though she was running out of patience with Isabelle. "It's spores from a kind of fungus that grows in the far woods. There's nothing of the black cat about it."

Fingering the bag now, Isabelle wondered. Couldn't Grete be just a little bit more magical than she was admitting? If so, Isabelle hoped she'd cast a spell on the kids at the camp, turn them into peace-loving hippies who believed in hugs, not homicide.

"Black-souled baby killer."

Okay. Enough was enough.

Isabelle turned around. "What babies? Name one baby." She put her hands on her hips. "Do you know one single baby from your village?"

Hen thought a moment. "Not from Corrin, no," she admitted finally. "But there are stories from Greenan and Drumanoo. Many a babe has gone missing from Greenan and Drumanoo."

"See?" Isabelle was pleading now, wanting Hen back on her side. Wanting to be friends again. "Don't you see? There are no missing babies. Only one missing child, and that was an accident that happened fifty years ago. There's no witch, Hen! No witch!"

Hen frowned. "You don't have to be *the* witch to be *a* witch, now, do you? I wouldn't wonder if you turned out to be a witch too, dropping in from another world the way you have, called here by your witch of a grandmother."

Isabelle decided to try another tack. Shifting her pack from her left shoulder to her right, she began walking again. "So we've never talked very much about my world, have we, Hen?" She threw out the question like she was lobbing a softball toward home plate. "It's never really come up much."

"I didn't know until this morning you were from another world, miss." Hen's tone was bitter, but she caught up with Isabelle and walked beside her. "Oh, I knew you were from someplace else, but I'd thought it was some province outside of the County of the Five Villages. Didn't know you'd dropped in from the clouds or wherever it is you're from."

"The way I got here was through my school," Isabelle said, deciding to ignore anything Hen said that was even a little sarcastic or unfriendly. "Through a door. I opened the door and fell down here—well, to the school in Greenan, to be precise. Which sounds odd and strange and unusual, I know."

"Not that strange," Hen muttered, kicking up a cloud of dust from the path.

"What was that?" Isabelle wasn't sure she'd understood.

"I said, it's not that strange," Hen repeated, more clearly this time. "I've heard stories. Falling in, they call it. You're not the only one who's ever done it."

Isabelle sighed and continued. "Anyway, I was very happy that I had—fallen in. Because life at my school was the tiniest bit lonely. But since I've been here, I haven't felt lonely at all, not with you and Grete—"

"I don't care to hear the witch's name," Hen snapped.

"She's not a witch—," Isabelle started to protest, then stopped herself. "Fine. You and my grandmother. So that's been nice. Nobody was ever very nice at my school. I tried to make friends, but I wasn't very good at it. Now I think it's because I'm a half changeling—"

"Hush, miss!" Hen hissed from behind her. Isabelle,

thinking that Hen was protesting that there was no such thing as a half changeling, and believing she could make a reasonable case that there was, turned to argue. But when she did, she saw that Hen was peering into the woods, one hand raised in Isabelle's direction, as if to stop any words that might be about to tumble out of Isabelle's mouth.

Hen, still looking left and right, edged closer to Isabelle. "We're being followed," she whispered. "I wouldn't be surprised if it's that witch grandmother of yours either."

In a flash, Hen scooped up a rock from the ground and pitched it into the woods. "I see ya, ya old cow!"

But the voice that yelped from behind the bushes was not that of an old cow or a young bull or any farmyard animal, and it was most certainly not that of Grete the Healer.

No, from the sound of it, it was the voice of a boy.

Wait a second.

Make that two boys.

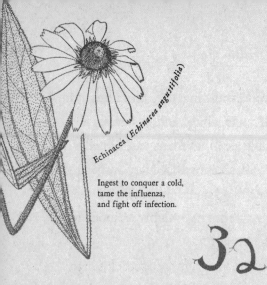

Echinacea (*Echinacea angustifolia*)

Ingest to conquer a cold,
tame the influenza,
and fight off infection.

32

Isabelle pointed at the redheaded boy as soon as he stepped out from behind a bush. "You're Samuel. From Greenan." She pointed at the other, taller boy. "And you're the rat-faced boy, but I never heard your name."

The rat-faced boy sneered at her. "And you're the witch's girl." He turned to Samuel. "I told you that's what was going on back there. See how she knows who we are without even asking? Witchy indeed."

"She knows who I am," Samuel corrected him. "She thinks you're a rat."

Hen stepped forward. "If you're from Greenan, what are you doing here?"

"And how's that your business?" Rat Face asked,

reddening. "We've the right to be here, whether you think it or not."

Samuel ignored his friend. "We've been checking up on that one." He waved his hand toward Isabelle. "Followed her when she left Greenan, tracked the both of you down Corrin way."

"We've had our eye on you, witch girl," Rat Face added.

"Just the first couple of days," Samuel corrected. "Followed your tracks to Corrin, watched the goings-on for a bit, and came back. Not much to see, unless leaf gathering interests you. Doesn't me, much. When we didn't catch sight of the witch, we wondered if she hadn't moved farther south and these woods were safe again for roaming. That's why we're out and about today. Our fishing gear's in the bush over there."

Not much of a secret keeper, old Sam. Isabelle decided she liked that about him. In fact, she found him generally likeable. In fact, what if he came with her to the camp? If she liked him—she who liked very few boys, almost none she could think of, certainly not Rat Face over there—then anybody would. If Isabelle surrounded herself with likeable people, then the children would listen to her. They would trust her. They'd be less likely to stone her to death when she told them the news.

"We're on our way to the camp north of Greenan," she said to Samuel. "I could use your help."

As Isabelle explained, she could see the interest on Samuel's face. Oh, sure, it was interest mixed with disbelief, a half cup of fear, a dash of confusion, but definitely interest.

Rat Face, on the other hand, laughed and rolled his eyes like yo-yos. "So you think your granny's not a witch, then? She's got you fooled, that one does."

Isabelle ignored him. "The sooner people know the truth, the sooner they can lead normal lives again," she told Samuel. "They won't have to be afraid of a witch anymore."

"*If* they believe you," Samuel amended. "There's no saying whether they will or won't. But I suppose I believe you, so I'll come. Quinn here, he'll come too."

Rat Face—Quinn—looked at his friend. "You believe her? You believe there's no witch? Just like that?"

Samuel shrugged. "Never much believed in the witch in the first place. Well, I did for a time, but lately I've been wondering. It's like she said"—he nodded toward Isabelle—"who do you know of that actually got killed? Always folks in the other villages, never Greenan."

"The only reason I'm going is to fetch my brothers and sister and take them back home," Hen declared. "That one"—she nodded toward Isabelle—"can do all the talking about witches she likes. I'll be no part of it."

Isabelle dropped back as the group began walking north. Why was Hen so stubborn? Why couldn't she get with the program, get over it, get real? Fact: There was no child-eating witch. Fact: This was good news. Why couldn't Hen accept it? Then she and Isabelle could go back to being friends. They could tell the news to the kids at the camp, drop off Hen's various siblings at home, then head back to

Grete's for a big "Everything's Okay Now" celebration.

Yeah, Isabelle thought. *Right*.

Catching up with the others, Isabelle was more than a little irritated to find Hen having a friendly conversation with Samuel (Hen, who had not said one friendly word to Isabelle all day), the two of them reminiscing about the different camps they'd been to over the years.

"You've been to the camps north of Greenan before, I suppose?" Samuel asked. "Too close to home for us during our season, of course, but I always snuck over there when the children came from other villages, watched 'em swing on the ropes over the creek."

"Aye, the ropes are good fun," Hen agreed. "Bet we'll find Jacob swinging on one when we get there. The only problem with the Greenan camp—no offense to you—is that the woods are frightening around the edges. You feel eyes peering in at you at night."

"All the camps are like that, not just Greenan,"

Samuel said. "Anyone will tell you that the woods around the whole of the Five Villages are alive. We go to Aghadoc in our season, and the little ones won't venture a foot from the campfire after darkness falls. When I was a wee boy, it didn't matter if it were light or dark, I spent a whole day feeling spooked."

"Then everyone will be even happier that there's no witch," Isabelle asserted. "We'll be bringing them good news."

Hen looked at Samuel. "You might want to be careful how you go about telling them about it," she said, ignoring Isabelle completely. "You being a stranger, they won't trust you much."

Samuel nodded in agreement. "We might do well to act the traveler at first, like folks looking for a place to stay. When they get used to us a bit, then we'll tell them. A day or two, and we'll know the best way to go about it, don't you think?"

"They'll be wondering why you kept it a secret from them," Rat Face pointed out. "They'll think you're not to be trusted."

Really, it was hard for Isabelle—who believed herself to be a peaceable person, but like most people had her limits—not to reach out and give Rat Face a hard pinch. But Samuel seemed to take Rat Face's idea seriously. "Let's think about it while we walk," he said. "And when we reach the camps, maybe the answer will set itself in front of us, in plain view."

But when they reached the camps, what they found was not an answer.

What they found was chaos.

33

Maybe you've been to summer camp. Remember the cozy cabins with their slightly funky, mildewy smell, the well-tended paths you followed from this activity (archery!) to that (lanyard making!) over the course of a morning? How could you forget the sparkling lake, the noisy, joyful mess hall, the s'mores, the sing-alongs? Oh, Michael, row that boat ashore, yes, indeedy.

Even if you've never been to camp, this is what you imagine camp is like, isn't it? Me too. The words that pop to mind are "idyllic," "frolicsome," "middle-of-the-night-giggles" (I know, I know, not a word, more a phrase, but you get my point). Happiness of the unfettered sort.

I want you to close your eyes and take your giant mental eraser and erase all those images. Can you do it? I know asking you to rid yourself of certain thoughts is almost as good as asking you to think those thoughts obsessively (whatever you do, don't think of pink elephants!), but do your best.

Because here's the thing: Your ideas of What Camp Is won't work for this story, sorry to say. The camp we're about to enter is of a different sort. It's a camp where children are doing their best to survive without their parents, the whole time fearful of a witch popping out of nowhere to carry them off and eat them for supper. To say that the littlest children have constant stomachaches would be an understatement.

Under the best of circumstances, the Greenan camp wasn't a wildly happy place, but because it was a camp filled with children, all was not gloom and doom. The Greenan camp was known especially for its three rope swings tied to trees at the edge of the creek, and on warm days the children flew over the water, shrieking and squealing, little sisters ignoring their big sisters' warnings, the tallest boys climbing as close to the tops of the ropes as they could.

And so it had been at the beginning of the witch's season, when the children had started to make their way into the camp, first in a trickle, then in a great stream of chatter and commotion. But two days before Isabelle first met Hen on the path to Corrin, a girl named Lanny entered the Greenan camp feeling dizzy and slightly out of sorts. She was ten, and normally the picture of health, and on this particular day she couldn't figure out why she felt so strange. Had the witch cast a spell on her? Or was it just the fear racing around her heart that caused the white dots to appear in front of her eyes?

No, not the witch, not the fear. It was influenza the girl carried with her into the camp, and it caused her to wobble on her feet and grab at branches to keep from falling. Within a day, half the children had caught it, and the other half were left to care for them. But how? Damp cloths on the forehead. Creek water boiled in a pot and dripped down their throats.

You know and I know those remedies couldn't possibly work against the flu. Nothing worked. And every day more children got sick, and so there were fewer children to act as nurses and gather food and keep the fires going.

And then one day somebody came. They had been praying for this, the children who still had their wits about them, who weren't roiling and writhing with fever and chills. They had been hoping for more than a week that somebody would come. Somebody who could save them.

And now, finally, they were here.

Boneset (*Eupatorium Perfoliatum*)

Take to douse
the flames
of high fever.

34

Isabelle felt it even before they walked into the camp. Not just felt it, but knew it, as in: A little piece of knowledge had somehow knit itself into her bones. She knew that they shouldn't go in there. Something was wrong.

Rat Face agreed. "Smells funny," he said at the edge of the clearing, from where they could see makeshift tents here and there, but not one single child. "Smells the way it did when Uncle Seth died. Like fever and rot."

Hen turned pale. "The little ones are in there," she said in a shaky voice. "Sugar, Artemis, Jacob, all of 'em."

"Then in we go." Samuel put a reassuring hand

on Hen's shoulder. "We'll find your little ones first, and then see what's to be seen about the others."

"Yes, we must find them," Hen agreed. She rubbed her hands hard against her arms, as though she were cold. "Oh, but won't Mam be after me if a single hair of their heads is out of place!"

"What if they're ill?" Rat Face moved so that he was blocking the way into the clearing. "What good will it do us to go near? We'll only become ill ourselves. There are stories, you know, of fever sweeping through a camp and death following fast behind. If we were to die, who would tell the story of the witch?"

"So you believe us now, do you?" Samuel asked his friend. "Had a change of heart?"

Rat Face shrugged. "Remains to be seen what I believe the case to be. Not enough evidence either way. But something's amiss here, no denying that." He turned to Isabelle. "You feel it, don't you?"

The strange thing: Not only did Isabelle feel it, she could hear it. Which is to say, she found one voice in her head, then another, and another, that were not hers. They toppled over one another—

O I'm so cold o there is a black dog that bites please run I can't run . . .

The coldest cup of water, Mother, if only you would . . .

I will sit up I will sit up and see about Mazie I will sit up in one more minute . . .

—in a jumble of nonsense that Isabelle recognized from the times she'd been sick with a fever, but the voices themselves were unfamiliar, kids' voices, kids who needed help now. And on top of them, her own thoughts insisting that she help them.

But her feet wouldn't move. She was supposed to help these kids and risk getting sick herself? Maybe even die? Was that fair? How would she get home if she died? Who would know what had happened to her?

A tiny voice wound its way above the others in Isabelle's head, announced itself clearly: *Help.*

Odd: It was Hen's voice. No, not exactly. More like Hen's voice if Hen had been three or four, Hen's voice made small and weak.

Sugar.

Isabelle sighed. She couldn't let Sugar die, could she? The little sister of her best friend (even if her best friend didn't want to be best friends with her)? She didn't think so. She pushed past Rat Face and began walking toward the clearing.

"We won't get sick if we wash our hands," she yelled back to the others, who all looked at her like she was crazy. *Haven't they ever heard of germs?* Isabelle thought irritably, and then realized that, no, they probably never had. "Washing cleans the sickness off you if you've touched it," she explained. "It's something we discovered back where I'm from. It's not one hundred percent guaranteed, but it seems to help a lot."

"And maybe if we dance around the mulberry tree three times, we'll never catch a cold," Rat Face replied.

"It does sound like foolishness," agreed Hen halfheartedly.

"It's science," Isabelle insisted. "You'll have to trust me on this one."

Samuel looked doubtful. "Where'd you say you were from?"

Isabelle pointed vaguely northward. "Up there. From a place where we've made a lot of scientific advances. Like vaccinations."

"Vaccinations?" Samuel asked, sounding interested.

Isabelle nodded, feeling very smart all of a sudden. "Vaccinations are medicine you take so you don't get sick. And we've got antibiotics, which cure you when you do get sick. But one of the most amazing scientific discoveries we've made"— and she said "we've" as though she herself had been on the research team that made it—"is that if you wash your hands, you get rid of some of the stuff that makes you sick in the first place. Germs go right down the drain."

"You're right," Samuel said, shaking his head. "We'll just have to trust you."

Hen took a deep breath. "Don't have much of a choice, I suppose."

Rat Face didn't say anything, but he followed the

rest of them into the camp. As they reached the center of the clearing, the voices swarmed thick in Isabelle's head, like she'd tuned into a hundred radio stations at once. She had to concentrate. Where was Sugar?

It came to her suddenly: near the big tree. Isabelle didn't know how she knew this, but she did, and she looked around her for the tallest tree at the edge of the clearing. "Sugar's in there!" she shouted, pointing to the tent beneath the tree.

They ran. It wasn't much of a tent, a piece of canvas held up by sticks and string. Hen was first in. "Oh, she's burning up!" she cried. "Sugar, I'm here. Hen is here."

"Hen!" a little girl's voice trembled. "I knew you'd come!"

Rat Face pushed Isabelle toward the tent. "Get in, then! See what it's all about!"

Isabelle crawled through the canvas opening. She found Hen cradling a little girl, bony-thin, dark hair damp with sweat, in her arms. Hen looked up at her. "She's got a fierce fever. I wish I knew how long it's been burning in her."

"Oh, days and days," Sugar said in a weak voice. "I'm so weary of it, Hen."

Hen stroked her hair. "What was I thinking, letting you run off? Why must I make a mess out of everything?"

"Where've you been, Hen? I've been lonesome for you."

"And me for you, but I'm here, I'm here. Now tell me where Jacob and Artemis and Callou and Pip are, and then we'll leave you for a bit of sleep."

"Artie and Callou and Pip are in the next spot," Sugar said, barely whispering. "Jacob's gone. We haven't seen him in ever so long. Almost as long as you, Hen."

Hen glanced at Isabelle, a frightened look in her eyes. "Where do you suppose he's gone?"

Isabelle shrugged. "Do you think he's gone to look for you?"

"Probably. Probably thought I got lost or fell and broke my leg," she said, and her face seemed to crumble. "How could I be so stupid, not heading straight for the camp when I was supposed to?"

Samuel opened the canvas flap and stuck his head in. "No time for that now. These children are sick nigh unto dying. We got to do something about it. You can have all your terrible thoughts later."

Hen nodded, and she and Isabelle climbed out of the tent. Samuel gestured toward the other tents. "They're all sick with the fever," he reported. "I don't know if there's a thing to be done other than to give 'em water and put cloths on their heads."

"What's to be done is to leave this place," Rat Face said. "What's the use of us all dying too?"

"There's got to be *something* that can bring the fever down." Isabelle turned to Hen. "Maybe if we found some—I don't know, some sort of something." She was sorry now she hadn't paid closer attention to Grete all those mornings out in the woods. "Do you know?"

"Comfrey tea might do it, or echinacea, if we could find some," Hen said eagerly, her face brightening. "We'd have to boil the flowers. There's no time to dry them."

Rat Face sneered. "You the witch, then? Sounds like it."

"What if I was one?" Hen faced him full-on, her hands on her hips. "What if I was to put a spell on you right on this spot?"

"Ain't you the kidder," Rat Face said, but his face had paled. "Last I heard, there weren't any witches."

"Still and no, I'd watch your back all the same," Hen warned.

It was decided quickly: Rat Face would fill as many buckets and pots as he could find with water from the creek, and Samuel would build a fire for boiling. Hen and Isabelle would search the woods for comfrey, boneset, and echinacea to boil into a tea to bring down the children's fevers. They would look for witch hazel, too, which Isabelle thought might work as a kind of antiseptic to clean their hands.

"What about your brother, then?" Samuel asked before they set off. "Should one of us go searching for him?"

"No time for it," said Hen. "Besides, if he left soon after he got here, then maybe the fever hasn't touched him. Just pray that he's safe wherever he is."

"Echinacea looks like purple daisies," Isabelle said, finally remembering something Grete had taught her. "Boneset is pink and lacy. I don't remember comfrey, though."

"Flowers like bluebells, only they're purple," Hen reminded her. "Triangular, notched leaves. Look for it around the edges of the clearing, in the sunny spots."

While they searched, the voices continued to sound in Isabelle's head, frightened voices, feverish voices. Was this her magic? Hearing voices?

Frankly, it wasn't what Isabelle would have picked. It was too noisy, for one thing. And for another, it was a little disconcerting.

But.

But.

If she could hear voices and thoughts, if this was her magic—

She had magic. She was magical!

She was Isabelle Bean, half changeling.

Just as she'd suspected all along.

35

The children!

There were forty-three of them in all, the oldest a thirteen-year-old boy named Peter, the youngest a toddler everyone called Woogie, though Isabelle was sure that couldn't be her real name. Not everyone had the fever. A group of twelve who were still well had moved their tents farther into the woods, hoping to be spared. They were led by an eleven-year-old named Elizabeth.

"At first we did what we could," she told Isabelle and Hen after spying them from her campsite and trailing them through the woods until she felt sure it was Hen from Corrin she'd sighted. Now the three girls sat on rocks at the creek's edge, pulling petals off the flowers Isabelle and Hen had collected. "Fed 'em broth, cooled their foreheads. But it didn't help, and more of us well ones were getting sick. If this is a killing fever, there's not much help to be given, is there? Unless this medicine works."

Isabelle could tell by the girl's voice that she was doubtful. She glanced at Hen, who was determinedly plucking away at the echinacea and boneset. "It'll work," Hen said through gritted teeth. "I'll make it work."

"I'll do what I can to help you," said Elizabeth. "But I won't nurse the sick ones anymore. I've got two little brothers still well. We don't have parents, so if I take fever and die, they're on their own. I'm not a coward, mind you, but I can't go leaving those boys by themselves. They're only five and three, and an especially foolish five and three at that."

"You can help make the teas," Hen told her. "Isabelle and me will take care of the sick ones."

They carried the leaves and petals and stems in their skirts to the clearing where Samuel had built the fire and Rat Face was bringing the first pot of water to boil. "Dump it all in the cauldron," he told them. "We'll begin our brewing."

Hen shook her head. "He's all talk and no brains, that one. We'll steep the echinacea first, see what a dose of that does to the fever."

Sugar got the first cup of the tea, twisting this way and that as Hen tried to spoon some of the hot liquid into her throat, but instead spilled it on Sugar's chin. "Come on, Sugar," Hen pleaded with her sister, wiping up the mess and trying again. "Take a sip to please Mam."

Sugar's eyes widened. "Is Mam here? Oh, I want to see her!"

"You'll see her soon enough, I promise. Now open your mouth for a sip of tea."

She looked up at Isabelle. "You best go to the others. Can't think to tell you where to begin. Just start at one end and work to the other, I suppose."

And so began the career of Nurse Isabelle Bean. She filled a cup with tea and walked to the far end of the campsite. But after a few steps she heard a child's voice calling, *Now, now, now, I need you now,* and it took her one second to realize (a) the voice was coming from inside her head (she supposed she should get used to that); and (b) the voice was from a child in that tent right over—where?—there.

"I'm here, I'm here," Isabelle called as she entered the tent, careful not to spill the tea she was carrying. A boy of seven or eight was sitting halfway up, his eyes closed.

"Ma, I been calling ya for days and days," the boy fussed, his words sounding parched, his head rocking this way and that. "My head hurts somethin' fierce, Ma. I think it's been cracked on with a hammer."

"It's the fever that's making your head hurt," Isabelle told him. "And I've got just the medicine for you." She moved next to the boy's pallet and kneeled down. "You think you can take a sip?"

The boy slowly opened his eyes. "Ya look different, Ma. Not like yourself at all."

"I'm not your mother," Isabelle admitted. "I'm Isabelle Bean. And I have some tea for you to drink that will make you feel better."

The boy rocked back. "Isabelle Bean? Why, who ever heard of such a one as an Isabelle Bean?"

"My mom, I guess." Isabelle refused to be offended. "And my grandmother, for another."

"Aye, that's good!" the boy replied before falling back onto his blanket and shutting his eyes again. He gave a sleepy giggle. "Yer ma and yer granny, they knows who you are, old Isabelle Bean."

Isabelle put her hand behind his head, lifting it a bit. "Drink this tea now, and later I'll tell you more funny things, okay?"

The boy obediently opened his mouth and took a sip. "'Tis bitter," he complained groggily.

"But good for you. Take another sip," Isabelle urged, and in a minute the cup was drained.

"You'll come back, won't you, Isabelle Bean?" the boy called weakly after her as she stood to leave. "My name's Luke. Pleased ta meet ya and all."

"I'll check on you after I see the other kids," Isabelle promised. "Now you go back to sleep."

Through the rest of the afternoon and into the

evening, Isabelle followed the children's voices, going to the most urgent ones first, and eventually all of them. The older children did as Isabelle told them, drank the tea in little sips until the cup was empty. The youngest ones struggled and squirmed, but Isabelle found she could distract them with funny little stories—

"Once upon a time, there was a purple man," she'd begin, and the child's eyes would widen and she or he'd say, "A purple man, really?" and Isabelle would say, "Take a sip and I'll tell you more."

—and the children would open their mouths like little birds, and Isabelle would carefully spoon in the tea. Some of the children called her Mam or Ma, and one little raven-haired girl named Cornelia insisted that Isabelle was Dorie Malone from down Drumanoo way. "Don't you remember me, Dorie? From Harvest Festival? We played ring-a-levio and Postman's Knock and won all the prizes."

"Oh, sure, now I remember," Isabelle told the girl, smoothing back her hair.

The girl smiled, her eyes unseeing. "Oh, I

thought you were the prettiest girl and the dearest thing ever, Dorie."

And then she fell asleep.

All the while, Isabelle paid attention to the voices. When she was focused on helping a child drink the tea, the voices faded into a hum of a buzz that tickled her brain ever so slightly, but when she left one tent to search out another, the buzz grew louder, the words becoming clear, one voice leaving just enough room for another to be heard.

The buzz. Isabelle remembered now where she'd first heard it. Days ago—weeks ago? years ago?—in Mrs. Sharpe's classroom, coming up through the floor. She'd thought it had come from the stove in the corner of the room where she'd first met Samuel. But now she realized it had come from the children.

Isabelle looked up at the sky. Was Hangdale Middle School on the other side of all that blue? Were there worlds on top of worlds on top of worlds everywhere you looked?

She thought there probably were.

And then she followed the voices to the next tent.

36

When she was done, Isabelle went to the creek to wash. She dipped her hands in the cool water and splashed it on her face. What time was it? She looked up and saw a handful of stars squinting shyly out of the darkening sky. *Seven o'clock,* she thought. *Maybe eight.*

"You'll be wanting this, I'll wager."

Startled, Isabelle turned. Elizabeth was standing on the bank behind her. She climbed down several large rocks and handed Isabelle a bundle of leaves and stems. "It's the witch hazel. Hen sent me out looking for it."

Isabelle carefully tore the leaves and stems into pieces and then rubbed them over her hands and arms. "Where I come from, they call this disinfectant. It gets the sickness off you."

Elizabeth squatted on the rock and peered at Isabelle. "I met a girl like you once. From the other world, she was, had queer notions, odd shoes, just like you."

So there had been others, just as Hen said. Isabelle Bean was not the first person to ever fall in.

"Where is she now?"

"Don't know," Elizabeth said. "Went home, I reckon. You plan on going home?"

Isabelle turned back to the creek and watched as the water jumped over the rocks in its rush to get downstream. "Sure," she said. "In a little while." Now that she knew she definitely had magic, she wanted to spend more time with Grete before she went back, pick up some hints and tips, the basic operating instructions.

"Don't you miss your folks? I miss my ma and da something fierce, but there'll be no going home to them until we meet in God's heaven. If they were still here on this Earth, I'd run home to them this very minute, witch or no."

Isabelle looked at Elizabeth. She wondered if the girl's thoughts would start streaming into her head, pouring out her cares and woes. But the only thoughts she heard were her own. Why was that? Was it because there was nothing that Isabelle could do to help Elizabeth? That's what all the voices had in common, wasn't it? They all needed help. But there wasn't anything she could do to get Elizabeth's parents back.

She stood and wiped her hands on her skirt. "Yeah, I want to see my mom, definitely. We've got a bunch of stuff to talk about. When the time's right, I'll go back."

Elizabeth stood too and climbed after Isabelle up the creek bank. "Well, you can't stay here forever. None of them that fall in do. It's not your time or place."

Isabelle considered this. She wanted to go home, but she didn't like being told she didn't have options. "Maybe I don't have a time or a place," she suggested. "Maybe I'm a floater."

"A floater?" Elizabeth sounded confused.

"A floater," Isabelle repeated, liking the sound of it. "You know, someone who floats through time and space, going from here to there, exploring."

Elizabeth was quiet for a moment. "Don't think there's such a thing," she said finally. "Everybody's got a time and a place. You leave it now and again, in dreams, or if you're drawing a picture and all wrapped up in your imagination—" She paused a second. "Do you know what I mean by that?"

Isabelle nodded. "That's a kind of floating too, I suppose."

"I think that's mostly the kind folks do. And then every once in a while, maybe, one or two do as you have, and fall into another world for a bit, but you can't stay. You've got to go back."

"But why?" Isabelle asked. "I'm not saying I won't, but why do I have to?"

Elizabeth touched Isabelle on the shoulder. "Because your ma misses you." She paused, then added softly, "She does, ya know. She hasn't much family other than you, has she?"

Isabelle stopped short. "How do you know?"

Elizabeth grinned. "You think you're the only one who has a bit of a gift, girl?"

"You mean magic?"

"Magic, gift, different words for the same thing. You know when folks need help, I know when folks need each other. 'Tis a simple gift, but sometimes useful."

And so the two girls continued walking toward the camp, one smiling, the other shaking her head.

37

Faint voices rang in Isabelle's ears. She shook her head, trying to make the voices fall out, and rolled from under the layers of blankets that made up her bed. "Bed" in quotes.

They had been in the camp three days, and Isabelle was exhausted. Some of the kids seemed to be improving, true enough, especially the younger ones, who were beginning to come out of their tents and take tentative steps this way toward the fire or that way to the creek. Sugar had grown well enough to help Rat Face tend to the brewing, and Isabelle noticed that he didn't seem half as cranky when he was making up riddles and rhymes to keep the little girl amused.

But a lot of the kids were still sick, and Hen and Isabelle were tending to them hour after hour, bringing them the teas, applying cool cloths to their foreheads, singing little songs. It felt to Isabelle like they had been there a hundred years and would be there a hundred years more, and she would never see Grete or her mom again, and there would never be a time to tell everyone there was no witch and they could all go home.

Isabelle dressed and made her way to the tent where Elizabeth was doling out the little bit of breakfast there was to be had. That was another problem: Food supplies were low.

"We'll have to move camp," Isabelle heard Samuel say as she walked into the tent, where Elizabeth was holding up a piece of bread in each hand, as if to show how little they had left. "We've barely enough to feed ourselves."

"The children aren't well enough to be moved," Elizabeth told him. "Besides, it's the season. We can't go back now—the witch would get us for sure."

Samuel turned to Isabelle, raised an eyebrow at her. "It's time, don't ya think?"

"To move camp?" asked Isabelle. "I don't know if that's even possible right now."

"No, no. Time to tell this one the truth," Samuel replied. "As the others get well, we'll tell them, too. But we can't stay here more than two or three more days before there's nothing left to eat."

Elizabeth shook her head sadly. "It wasn't planned well, that's the truth of it. Witch came upon us unawares. We didn't expect the signs till much later in the spring, so when the shadow crossed the moon, no one was ready. Usually we come in with plentiful flour and soda for bread, our packs filled with potatoes. But there wasn't time this season. She's got us trapped now, that witch does."

And so Samuel and Isabelle told Elizabeth about the witch, the non-witch, the complete absence of a witch in the woods. She listened closely, then said she had to think about it and walked in circles around the camp for an hour before returning and saying, "Not everyone will believe you, you know," before beginning to chop mushrooms to put in a soup for lunch. "You'll have a hard time with this crowd, convincing them."

"Have we convinced you?" Samuel asked. "That would be a start."

"Don't know yet," said Elizabeth forthrightly. "I'd like some proof."

Isabelle and Samuel looked at each other. "Bring your grandmother here," Samuel said, and Isabelle nodded. In fact, why hadn't they thought of that as soon as they came into a camp where everyone was sick? Why hadn't one of them run to retrieve the famous Grete the Healer?

"It's a risk," Samuel said, as though reading Isabelle's thoughts (could he? she wondered, feeling at that very second a little weary of thought reading and voice hearing and magic and gifts in general). "But perhaps one well worth taking."

It was decided: Isabelle and Samuel would go. Isabelle ran to tell Hen, who was at the campfire overseeing the brewing of a batch of echinacea tea. She agreed she could keep watch over the children with Rat Face and Sugar's help, so Isabelle and Samuel started off, carrying several burlap bags apiece to fill from Grete's stores of flour, sugar, apples, and nuts.

"I know your grandmother's not the witch," Samuel said after they'd gone a mile or two down the path toward Corrin, "but still and the same, it makes my bones quiver a bit to be walking in her direction."

"Maybe if you remind yourself there was never a witch to begin with, you won't be so scared," Isabelle offered.

Samuel puffed out his chest. "I'm not scared," he said. "Just a bit wary, is all. Grew up my whole life believing in a witch, you know."

"But now you know there's not a witch, so why worry about it?"

"Habit, I reckon," Samuel replied with a shrug.

It was a warm morning, a few clouds in the sky, a handful of sparrows flitting through the trees over their heads. After days spent in stuffy tents, Isabelle enjoyed being outdoors. She could smell honeysuckle and thought she might grab some if she saw it. Grete could make some honeysuckle tea, and maybe some cookies, or a cake, a couple gallons of soup. . . .

Isabelle's stomach growled.

"I could use something to eat myself," Samuel agreed, and plucked a piece of grass from the side of the path to chew on.

After they'd walked for an hour, Isabelle heard something strange, and then realized it wasn't what she was hearing that was strange—it was the fact she didn't hear anything at all. No voices crowded her head, no moans and groans jostled for a place near the front of her brain. It was quiet as a garden at night in there, only the occasional chirp of one of Isabelle's own thoughts disturbing the air.

Isabelle smiled. It was nice to have a break. Maybe when she'd had more practice at being magic, she'd be able to control the noise in her head a little better, organize it, give each troubled thought its own little room in her brain. Maybe, too, she could learn how to pick up happy thoughts. Why limit herself to cares and woe? It might get depressing after a while, if all she heard were people's problems. How about their wishes? What if she could learn the sort of magic that would help her make wishes come true? Could a half changeling do that? Or was the wish-granting market cornered by fairies?

But for now, sweet silence, a beautiful spring morning, a walk through the woods, every step taking them closer to food—

Isabelle came to a sudden stop.

Something was in her head.

It was a voice so faint as to be a hundred miles away, at the farthest, darkest, most distant part of Isabelle's thoughts. It took her a minute, but then she recognized it. Grete. Grete was in trouble. Isabelle froze, panicked. She could feel it, feel the pain in her bones, the dizziness swirling around her brain. Grete was sick. Grete was—

No. No, no. Isabelle's heart thumped against her rib cage. Her breath was trapped in her lungs. Nothing bad could happen to Grete, Grete who was not a witch, but a healer, Grete who took care of people, Grete who needed Isabelle, Grete who wanted everyone to know the truth—

Grete who was Isabelle's grandmother.

"We have to run!" Isabelle grabbed Samuel's hand and pulled hard. "Fast! Now!"

"Where?" cried Samuel, already moving, already breaking into a sprint. "What?"

"Run!" came Isabelle's only reply. "Run!"

Like lightning, like wind, like their feet were on fire—

They ran.

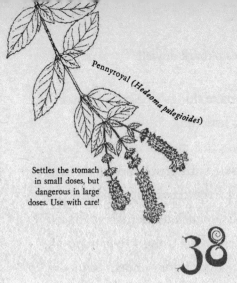

Pennyroyal (*Hedeoma pulegioides*)

Settles the stomach in small doses, but dangerous in large doses. Use with care!

38

Now, you don't know Jacob, and neither did Isabelle or Samuel, or Grete for that matter. So how could you tell just by looking at him that he could make such a mess out of things?

Answer: You couldn't.

Oh, little boys. Eight-year-old boys, boys old enough to come up with elaborate plans, young enough to completely flub them.

But imagine poor Jacob. There he is, on the way to the Greenan camp, running off from Hen, a total lark—honestly, he had no intention of actually losing her. Hen was always in trouble with Mam as it was, the way she let the boys wrestle in the mud and couldn't for the life of her put a braid in Sugar's hair.

Jacob didn't want to make things worse for Hen. He just wanted to have a little fun.

So he reaches camp, sends off little Pip (only two, but amazingly self-sufficient) and Sugar and Artemis and Callou to the creek to play with the others, sets up the tents—without Hen's help, thank you very much (if there's one thing Hen's good at, it's putting up tents and tying knots, outdoors things; it's only with kids that she's hopeless), and where *is* that Hen, anyway?—and counts the blanket rolls, one for each. Every few minutes he looks up expectantly, sure that Hen will be standing right behind him, her arms folded across her chest, ready to box his ears for leaving her behind.

But there's no Hen, and there's no Hen, and then again, no Hen. Two hours, four hours, and then all the little ones getting nervous, like little chicks who've lost their ma.

Jacob had sat up half the night waiting, and by morning it was clear to him what had happened: They'd left Hen behind, and the witch had nabbed her! Not a doubt in his mind about it, and now it was up to Jacob to save Hen from certain doom. As soon as the morning broke across the horizon, Jacob was off to the woods, in search of the witch's lair.

How easy it had been to find it too! Well, maybe "easy" was the wrong word, if you counted the blisters that had brought his hike to a halt only two hours out of camp, what he got for so much walking about in two days' time, he supposed. He'd stopped by the creek's edge to soak his feet and had fallen asleep, and by the time he woke up and recalled what he was doing, the sky was already growing dark. And maybe "easy" doesn't describe the second day either, when he'd gotten terribly lost and after a half day's hike realized he was back at the Greenan camp. He peeked through some bushes to see if Hen was about, and when it was clear she wasn't, he moved on.

It was a fortunate thing that Jacob was the son of a traveling peddler and that he'd spent more than one summer sporting about from town to town with his father. He knew how to find food in the woods and where to find the freshest water and how to steal a cooling pie off a windowsill when need be. All these skills came in handy as Jacob became more and more lost in the County of the Five Villages, stumbling into Drumanoo and Aghadoc and then finding himself on the outskirts of Corrin after five days. Lucky then that he knew a good mushroom from a poison one and could recognize the tail end of a ramp sticking out of the dirt. One yank and dinner was served. After five days of a mushroom and onion diet, however, he was tempted to go home. Then he thought of how mad his mam would be if he showed up without the others and kept going.

It was on the eighth day of his misbegotten journey, following the creek north again, that he came upon the house in the woods, saw the old woman through the window, and knew he'd at last found the witch. What kind of old woman lived in the woods by herself, he wondered, except a witchy one? He looked up in the trees for the nets filled with bones, and felt almost entirely, positively, halfway sure he saw two of them hanging from the highest branch of a twisted elm. Yes, he had most certainly found the witch, and the hairs on his arm prickled with the news.

And what did he see there, on the porch? Wasn't that Hen's blue apron fluttering from the banister like a flag? Jacob squeezed his hands into fists.

Hen was here. He would save her.

Now, a less disciplined boy than Jacob would have run in right away brandishing a stick and yelling like a banshee for the old witch to give him back his sister. But Jacob was more cunning than that. He waited at the edge of the woods, passing the time by braiding vines into rope, and thirty minutes past the time the last light in the witch's house was dimmed, he crept in as silently as a slithering snake.

It was nothing to tie the witch to her bed, twisting and turning the vines, knotting them here and there. Oh, it helped that she'd been asleep when he started, true enough, but she'd awakened after two passes of the rope and put up a struggle, for sure. Too bad for the witch that she was old and he was young, and besides, Jacob was sitting on top of her the whole time. Like a rock, his da had said about him, and Jacob reckoned that was so. So what could the old hag do except ask—when it was all done and she was tied tight to her bed—what in the blue blazes did he think he was up to?

"Tying you to your bed, ya old hag," he'd happily informed her as he tugged at a final knot. "Ya tell me the whereabouts of my sister, I'll consider letting you go, but I'll only be considering it, mind you."

The old witch had squirmed, testing the strength of the rope, and finding she was no match against Jacob's superior knot tying, sighed. "Hen isn't here. She's gone to the Greenan camp with Isabelle."

Jacob staggered back a few steps. "Did I say her name was Hen or are you reading my thoughts?"

"You're the very picture of her, even in the dark," the witch insisted. "I'd know you were Hen's brother if I met you on the streets of the moon."

Jacob glanced around the room for a mirror but found none. Was it true he looked just like Hen? He thought Hen rather pleasant-looking, and he wouldn't mind resembling her a bit in a boylike way, he supposed, not that he cared a whit what he looked like.

"Where is she?" he asked again, remembering his mission. "You best be telling me, or I'll make you more the miserable for holding your tongue."

The witch sighed even more loudly. "I've told you where she is. Now cut this rope, and I'll get you something to eat, even if it is the middle of the night."

At the mention of eating, Jacob's stomach growled. He'd not eaten since the morning, and now the thought of food overwhelmed him. What could it hurt to untie the witch? he wondered. He'd keep close guard, let her fix him something to eat, and then back to the ropes it was, unless she led him directly to Hen.

"You best not be planning any witchy tricks," Jacob told the witch as he began pulling at the first knots. "You've not met up with the likes of me before. I'll have your hide if you try anything."

"Oh, I'm sure of it," the witch agreed, though

Jacob wasn't convinced she meant it. No matter, she'd learn soon enough if she tried any backhanded business, just as soon as he untied the knots. . . .

The job proved undoable. When Jacob tried cutting through the knots with a knife, he found the vines were too green to slice or pinch or pull apart. He didn't know whether to be impressed with himself or out of sorts. Out of sorts, he decided two days later, as he was fixing another bowl of soup for the witch, which he'd have to feed her himself. He couldn't let her die now, could he, or he'd never know Hen's whereabouts.

"Just tell me if you've killed her," he'd demanded on the morning of the fourth day, even though he knew he wouldn't get an honest answer. If the witch admitted to any witchery, he'd stop feeding her, and then where would she be? A dried-out, dead witch starved to death in her own bed, that's where. No, it would be nothing but lies from this one, but he couldn't keep himself from asking anyway.

"Why would I kill Hen?" the witch replied. "I've taught her everything I know. She's like a daughter

to me. Now go pull a book from the shelf and read
it aloud. I'm bored to bits lying abed all the day
long."

It hadn't been the first time she'd made the
request. "What—and cast a spell on my very own
self?" Jacob replied, just as he had before. "I don't
think I will, thank you very much."

But this morning, instead of letting the
subject drop, as she had every other time, the witch
looked at Jacob long and hard. "You can't read, can
you?"

Jacob frowned. Of course he could read, he just
chose not to unless it was absolutely necessary. He
had to squint to read, or else the letters were fuzzy,
and squinting gave him a headache. And was it his
fault that sometimes words got twisted around,
T-R-E-E written on the board looking like T-E-
R-R to him, and all the others laughing at his mistake? Well, he wasn't going to be a schoolteacher,
like that pig-nosed Mr. Wearall, so what did it matter anyway?

"Fine," the witch said when she saw she'd get no

response from him. "Then go pull some potatoes out of the root cellar and roast them. You look like you need something other than bread and soup to eat."

Really, Jacob was turning into quite a cook. The witch would yell instructions to him from her room, and he'd put together a nice meal of green tea soup and soda bread for the both of them. He was rather pleased with himself, he who had never cooked at home, cooking being a girl's job. But he'd always liked to watch Mam cook, and as it turned out, he'd picked up a trick or two.

"I wouldn't mind some pie, would you?" the witch called when Jacob returned from the cellar with an armful of potatoes. "There are dried apples in the cupboard and a bit of cinnamon I've been saving. It's a rare thing, here, to have cinnamon. It comes from far away. Do you know what it looks like? You'll find it on the top shelf."

If words get fuzzy and twist around in front of your eyes, it's a difficult thing to stand on a step stool and differentiate between this jar and that, the various labels blurring before your eyes. Now, Jacob had seen cinnamon before and knew it to be a reddish brown, but his mam never had used it (his father had carried it in his peddler's pack now and again, which is how Jacob knew about it). Still and all, there was a jar of brownish red leaves, a little minty smelling to be sure, but Jacob felt sure that was it. He didn't find the apples where the witch had said they were, but instead two cupboards over. Leave it to a witch, he thought, to mislead him even when he was doing her the favor of making a pie.

The witch gave him careful instructions for simmering the apples over a low flame and forking lard into a bowl of flour to make the crust. In an hour's time the pie was ready. Jacob smelled its apple-y smell and approved. He would have some after a dinner of roasted potatoes and dandelion greens from the garden, seasoned with a touch of spring onion.

The witch, however, wanted hers the very minute Jacob pulled it from the oven. "Don't you want it to cool?" he'd asked. "I know how to set a pie on the windowsill. Seen it done a thousand times."

"What? And let the birds have it? No, boy, bring me a piece right now. I take my pleasures as they make their presence known."

It was the very first bite that sickened her. "Bring me the jar of cinnamon," the witch demanded, her eyes widening when Jacob handed it to her. "This is pennyroyal, not cinnamon, boy. You've gone and poisoned me." She sounded more amazed than angry. She looked Jacob straight in the eye and asked, "Did you mean to?"

Jacob felt as though he'd been hit in the stomach. No, of course he hadn't meant to. Yes, yes, she was a witch, but she was an awfully nice witch, and he even believed her when she said she hadn't killed Hen.

"Quit blubbering, boy, and try to help," the witch commanded, her skin growing paler by the second. "Outside, in the thicket near the front gate, look for a shrub with white flowers and purple berries. Dark purple, almost black. Bring the berries to me right away."

Jacob stumbled out the front door and down the

steps, his eyes blinded with tears. Where was it? Where was the shrub? He swiped at his eyes with the back of his hand and looked and looked, but he couldn't find it. From inside the house the witch moaned.

White flowers, purple berries, it had to be here somewhere. She wouldn't lie to him about that, would she, not when she was poisoned and needed help. Jacob began pulling up plants willy-nilly, as though he might find the bush he was looking for by getting rid of all the bushes he wasn't looking for. Thorns scraped at his skin and vines tripped him up. Where was that stupid shrub?

"I'm sorry!" Jacob cried out. He fell to the ground and buried his head in his hands. Oh what, oh what had he done? "I'm sorry!" he cried again.

But there was no reply.

39

Isabelle and Samuel raced into Grete's yard, panting and holding their sides. Slowing, steadying themselves with their hands on their knees, taking in gulping, gasping breaths, it took a few seconds before they noticed the boy by the front gate.

"I've killed her," he called out forlornly. "I killed her, but I honestly didn't mean to. She was a nice old witch for a witch."

They dashed up the porch steps and through the door. Grete lay still on her bed, held to it by a hodge-podge of vines. Isabelle spun around, wanting to throttle the boy, throw something at him—how dare he tie Grete up! What could he have been thinking? Heat flashed from her fingertips to the roots of her hair.

Samuel waved his hand to get Isabelle's attention. He nodded toward Grete. "She's not dead yet,
but listen to her breathing, all hollow-like and raspy
that way. If she don't get help, she'll be dead soon.
We need to know what happened."

Isabelle bolted to the yard. "What did you do to
her?" she demanded of the boy, her heart pounding
so hard in her chest she thought it might push her
over into the grass.

"Put the wrong thing in her pie," the boy said.
"Didn't mean to. Thought I was putting in cinnamon, but instead it was pennies."

"Pennies?" Isabelle stared at him, then asked
again. "Pennies?"

"Pennies-something," the boy said. "Royal pennies, like a king might give you."

"Pennyroyal?"

The boy nodded excitedly. "That's the one!
Pennyroyal." His face turned glum again. "Thought
it was cinnamon. 'Twas the color of cinnamon."

Isabelle began to tremble, and he reached out a
hand to help her sit. "Hen should have come instead

of me," she said in a shaky voice, lowering herself to the ground. "She'd know what to do."

The boy looked at her, eyes wide. "You know Hen?"

Isabelle stared back at him. "Of course I know Hen. Do you?"

"Why, she's my sister!" he exclaimed. "Have you seen her?"

"Jacob!" Isabelle exclaimed. "Hen's been worried sick about you! Oh, I wish she were here. She'd know what to do about Grete. There's just got to be something we—"

"The shrub, she said."

"The shrub who said?"

Jacob pointed to the house. "The witch. She said there's a shrub out here with white flowers and purple berries. She wanted me to get her some, but I couldn't find it."

Isabelle leaped toward the front gate. "White flowers?" she called back over her shoulder. "Purple berries?"

"That's right," Jacob replied, sprinting after her

to the thicket. "I reckon it's something to make the poison not so poisonous in her belly."

"Or to make her throw up the pennyroyal," Isabelle suggested, crawling through the tangle of bushes and vines, ignoring the rocks that dug into her knees. "Throwing up is exactly what Grete needs to do!"

Jacob turned a bit green at that, but he began pushing through the vines and growth, grabbing at every plant in his way. "Hen could help with this?"

"Your sister is a natural-born healer," Isabelle informed him, pulling a thorny vine from her sleeve and tearing through a patch of flowering chamomile. "Grete taught her all sorts of things about plants and medicine."

Samuel came out to the porch. "She's still breathing, but she looks terrible gray," he called. "I wish Hen were here to look at her."

"I could go get her," Jacob volunteered. "I run fast."

"It'll take hours," Samuel pointed out. "I don't know if this one's got hours."

Isabelle stood up with a shout. "I found it!" She held up a bunch of branches and waved them at Samuel and Jacob. Scrambling over the thicket, she stumbled toward the cottage, her arms and legs scratched and bleeding, twigs tangled in her hair. She plucked off a purple-black berry from one of the stems. "This is what Grete said would help her! She can take these, and then when Hen gets here we'll figure out what to do next."

"I should go, then?" Jacob asked eagerly, moving toward the clearing. "It might help?"

"It might," Isabelle told him. "But hurry!"

He was already gone, his feet crashing over rocks and sticks.

Isabelle bounded up the porch steps, cradling the branches in her arms. "All Grete has to do is eat these. That's all she has to do."

"She's not even awake," Samuel pointed out. "I don't know how we can get them down her throat without choking her."

"We'll find some way," Isabelle insisted, sounding more confident than she felt. "We have to."

40

The next part of this story is a blur. How can I describe a blur to you? Maybe I can't. Maybe you should just close your eyes and think of clouds and, holding that thought, turn round and round and round.

Do you feel blurry yet?

Do you feel slightly ill and rushed and a touch out of sorts? A tad confused? Spin some more. Go faster, and while you do—

Take that picture of Grete you have in your mind. You've been reading about her for pages and pages now, so I know you have a picture. But it's a picture of someone up and moving about, isn't it? Someone lively and full of life? Well, change all that. Picture her lying down, unconscious, very sick, dying, almost dead.

And then spin around some more.

You know, I'm not actually a trained storyteller. They have schools for storytellers in which they learn the tricks for describing these things, but I don't want you just to see it, I want you to feel it, too, and I wonder if that's something they can teach you at storytelling school. You've come this far, traveled more than a few miles, and you deserve a place of honor in the middle of these next scenes, right there in the center of the room, invisible of course, but watching it all and feeling it all, being caught up in the blur and the fear and the racing hearts—

Keep spinning.

Keep spinning—

41

Isabelle's head was spinning and her eyes blurred with tears as she mashed the berries with her hands. But she refused to cry. No time for crying, no time to find the heavy pestle Grete used for crushing leaves and stems into a mush. No time for spoons or forks. Purple juice stained Isabelle's fingers, ran down her arms. She didn't know how many berries they needed, so she'd thrown all of them in the bowl, and now they were lumped together in a purple, juicy soup that jumped halfway up to her elbows each time she mashed down.

"Wake up, old woman," Isabelle heard Samuel yell from Grete's room. She could hear his knife tearing through the vines. "You need to wake up now!"

She hurried down the hall with the bowl of mush, trying not to spill, wishing as hard as she knew how that her hands would stop trembling. She'd never been so shaky, felt so helpless. When this was over and done with, she would learn everything in the world there was to know about healing herbs and plants, and then the next time someone was poisoned or deathly ill or had the slightest bit of tickle in their nose, the barest hint of fever, she'd be prepared. No more swirling, dizzy Isabelle, her hands a mess of mush.

By the time Isabelle reached the door, Samuel had untied Grete, but she was still unconscious. "She won't wake up," he reported. "I shook her and shouted at her, but her eyes won't open."

"Sit her up so her head's leaning back against the wall," Isabelle ordered, setting the bowl down on the table next to Grete's bed. She was guessing what to do. She hoped that at any second Samuel would take charge and start shouting out instructions, but Samuel looked as lost as Isabelle felt.

"You sit next to her and hold her," Isabelle

continued. Her throat tightened, but she forced herself to sniff back her tears. No time, no time! Besides, when had Isabelle Bean ever been a crybaby? Been afraid of anything (besides snakes, and practically everybody was afraid of snakes)? There was no time to wilt like a lettuce leaf. Isabelle took a deep breath, straightened her spine. "Tilt her head back, and I'll spoon the stuff in her mouth," she said, trying to sound less wobbly than she felt.

Samuel nodded. *He looks like he's going to be sick,* Isabelle thought as she dipped the spoon into the berries. She thought this thought in a clinical sort of way, deciding to ignore the goings-on in her own guts, the churning and swirling, the acidy dance—

No. No time for that. Dip the spoon in the bowl. No trembling. No shaking. Just dip and lift to Grete's mouth.

Isabelle did what she told herself to do. Her fingers only wobbled a little bit, her stomach only lurched halfway up her throat. The spoon slipped easily into Grete's mouth, past her teeth, over her tongue. "Sip it all, Grete, the whole thing," Isabelle whispered, and Samuel tilted Grete's head back to help the juice down her throat.

Again, the spoon over the lips and past the teeth. Down the throat. "Give her some water, don't ya think?" Samuel asked calmly, as though he did this sort of thing every day, as though he weren't scared to death too. He handed Isabelle a cup, and she tilted it above Grete's mouth, poured some water in. Grete coughed, sputtered, swallowed.

"That's the trick," Samuel exclaimed, just as Grete's stomach lurched. He quickly turned her on her side, held her head over the bowl he'd placed by her pillow. Grete heaved, and Samuel held on.

Isabelle held on to the bedpost, dizzy again, her head a swirl of noise, no words, just rush and buzz and tremble. Her knees buckled, but she caught herself, yanked herself up.

"More," she told Samuel after he'd pulled Grete back to a sitting position and wiped her mouth with his sleeve. "We've got to get it all out."

So they did it all again, and again, and after the last spoonful, the last hurl of purple mush, Grete's

eyes opened. She didn't say anything for a few minutes, just lay there breathing, her eyes darting back
and forth between Isabelle and Samuel.

"There's an awful side to it," she whispered when
she was finally able to speak. She lifted her head up
to take a sip of water from the cup Samuel offered.
"To this healing business. A dark and terrible side.
But I knew you wouldn't be afraid."

Isabelle slumped into the chair next to the bed.
Not afraid? Not afraid of mashing berries or spooning mush, maybe, or even of holding Grete's shoulders as the poison rushed out of her. She wasn't
afraid of doing what needed to be done.

No, it wasn't the doing that made Isabelle afraid.
It was the watching. Bad enough that Grete might
die—but to watch Grete die? To sit there and watch
as the life drained out of her face and hands?
Isabelle's brain reeled at the thought.

Grete reached over and touched Isabelle's hand.
"Everyone's afraid of that, girl. The worst thing, to
watch a bad death."

The world blurred in front of Isabelle's eyes.

Blurred and went spinning like it had been pushed off its axis—spinning into nothingness, blackness—

"But I'm not dead," Grete reminded her in a raspy whisper of a voice. "A bit worse for the wear, mind you, but not dead."

"You done good," Samuel said to Isabelle. "Good as Hen would have done, I'd wager."

She looked to the window, wishing Hen would appear. Grete wasn't dead, but Isabelle knew there was more to do. How do you heal a stomach torn up by poison? Isabelle hadn't the slightest idea, not a clue. Hen would have to take over from here.

It was early the next morning when the buzz began again in Isabelle's ears. She'd been sitting with Grete, dozing off for short stretches, then waking to give Grete sips of water. She and Samuel had spent the night before cleaning up mush and muck and bile in a tub in the kitchen, having wiped the floor with rags and taken the spoiled sheets off Grete's bed and exchanged them for clean ones. When they'd finally finished, Samuel had lain down on a pallet of blankets at the foot of Grete's bed and fallen into a hard, deep sleep. Isabelle sat in the chair next to Grete's bed and kept watch until her eyes wouldn't stay open any longer.

At first the buzz wove its way into Isabelle's dreams without disturbing her at all. Her head had been so full of strange noises and happenings all day, the buzz wasn't enough to catch her attention. But when she woke up, the buzz was still there. She turned quickly to Grete to see if she was breathing. When she was sure the old woman was fine, Isabelle stood, careful not to wake her, and walked to the porch.

The yard was empty. Still, the buzz grew louder in Isabelle's ears. She sat down in a rocker and waited. The yard slowly filled with light. The buzz grew even louder. Isabelle kept waiting.

Hen was the first to crash through the woods into the yard. "Is she dead?" she cried when she saw Isabelle. "Jacob said she was half-dead when he left here."

"She's alive," Isabelle reported, practically dropping out of her chair with relief at the sight of Hen. "She's in the bedroom. Try not to wake her up, though. She's pretty beat."

Hen ran up the porch steps, nearly stumbling in her hurry to get through the door. The buzz grew louder. Isabelle turned expectantly toward the woods, and sure enough, here came Jacob, with Rat Face behind him, holding Sugar in his arms.

"Is she still alive?" Jacob called across the yard. "Did the berries work?"

"They worked, they worked," Isabelle told him. "Boy, did they ever."

"Is this where the witch lives?" Sugar asked sleepily. "Jacob says she's a nice witch, but I never heard of a nice witch, have you?"

Isabelle stood and walked out into the yard. "She's not a witch. Jacob, you didn't go back and tell everyone you found a witch, did you?"

"Told 'em I found the very witch we'd been hearing about all these years, but that she wasn't bad at all. Pretty friendly, actually," Jacob said, sounding pleased with this bit of diplomacy. "Told 'em they didn't have a thing in the world to be scared about with this here witch, not a thing."

But Isabelle felt the chill of fear close over her, and when she looked to the edge of the yard, she saw a dozen or so kids from the camp standing at the edge of the woods—she could see Elizabeth and Luke and Cornelia and some of the others she'd nursed, little and big, all standing in the warm light of the morning, shivering and hollow eyed, most of them with sticks in their hands.

"They came with you?" Isabelle asked, turning to Rat Face, who nodded. "But why?"

"Heard about the witch and wanted to see for themselves. Some of 'em want to do more than just see her." He gently set Sugar down. "They want to have at her, if you catch my meaning. Jacob's been trying to talk 'em out of it, but they won't listen."

"Elizabeth?" Isabelle called. "Elizabeth, what are you doing?"

"We just want to make sure that witch can't do any more harm."

"But you know she's not a witch," Isabelle insisted. "Samuel and I explained it."

Elizabeth entered the clearing, a large branch in her hand. "But you're her granddaughter. Why would you tell the truth about her? Too much of a risk to believe you, I decided."

Just when you think you know somebody, Isabelle thought, fighting the panic rising inside of her. "But why wouldn't you believe Samuel?"

Elizabeth eyed Isabelle coldly. "You're both strangers to me. And you've got witchy gifts, don't you?"

Isabelle's mouth fell open. "But so do you! You knew that my mom misses me!"

"It's what you wanted to hear," Elizabeth said with a shrug. "Anybody could have guessed that about you."

As the two girls were talking, the other children had gathered behind Elizabeth, and they now formed a small army. Isabelle didn't know if she could defend herself against them. She thought suddenly of the packet of spores Grete had given her before she'd left for the camp. Where was it? She'd carried it back with her, she was almost positive.

Elizabeth moved toward Isabelle. "I want to see this witch for myself. And I want you to get out of my way."

Isabelle stood where she was. She looked past Elizabeth to the others. "You look a lot better, Luke," she said. "How's your head feel?"

"Ah, ya know, pretty good an' all," he told her. He started to say something else, but Elizabeth glared at him and he shut his mouth.

"Cornelia?" Isabelle called to the little girl who'd once thought she was her dearest friend Dorie. "Did you drink your tea before you left camp?"

Cornelia nodded, then looked down at the ground. The branch she carried wasn't much, more like a twig. Isabelle tried to imagine her using it to kill Grete. Ridiculous. Preposterous. Absolutely ridiculous—

In a flash, Elizabeth was trying to push past, butting Isabelle sideways with her shoulder. Isabelle barely managed to stay on her feet. She had to think fast. How could she stop this girl and her stick and all the other kids and their sticks? She needed a stick—no, a tree, a forest—

"She's sick!" she cried out in desperation. "If you go in there, you'll wake her up!"

Rat Face came and stood beside her. "Like that'll stop this lot," he muttered under his breath, but shoulder to shoulder with Isabelle he helped make a wall against the invaders. "Why can't you leave an old woman be?" he said to the others. "She's half-dead inside there."

"Like you were, remember?" Isabelle pleaded. "If she's a witch, how could she be so sick? Hen's in there giving her tea, just like we gave tea to you to bring down your fevers. Remember?"

"Has she got a fever, then?" a boy who looked about nine asked. "Does she have what we had?"

Jacob stepped forward. "Actually, I poisoned her. Completely by mistake. Didn't mean to; it just happened."

"You poisoned her because you knew she was a witch," Elizabeth hissed.

"Nah, I was trying to make a pie. Wasn't trying to put poison in it. Read the label wrong, is all." Jacob looked embarrassed. "Honest mistake, anybody could make it."

Luke raised his hand. "Could we see her? I mean, not to kill her or nothing. Just to see how she is? 'Cause I never heard of a witch being sick. Feel sorry for her, if it's true. I ain't never felt so bad in my life, way I did with that fever."

"Put down your sticks, and I'll take you inside," Isabelle told everyone. "But you have to be quiet. She needs to sleep."

"I slept for days and days when I was sick," Sugar said, making it sound like it had been years since she'd had the fever. "And I never heard of a witch who got sick either."

"Witches don't get sick," said Isabelle, reaching out one hand to Luke and the other to Cornelia, who'd dropped her pitiful twig in the grass. She didn't know if this was true or not, but it made sense. "That's how we know Grete's not a witch."

"Or if she is, she's a nice one," Jacob said affably.

Isabelle turned and gave him the finger across the throat sign. *Cut it out,* she mouthed. *Ix-nay on the itch-way.*

Jacob might have had trouble with labels, but pig Latin he read without any problem. He nodded at Isabelle and mimed zipping his lips.

Rat Face held out his hand to Elizabeth. "Branch, please. No weapons past the front gates."

With great reluctance, Elizabeth handed him her stick. "But leave it on the porch," she ordered. "I might need it later."

Entering Grete's room, the children lined up quietly against the walls. Hen sat in the chair next to the bed, cooling Grete's forehead with a damp cloth. Samuel stood on the other side of the bed, holding a steaming mug. When Hen saw everyone, she held a finger to her lips.

"She's very ill. You mustn't disturb her," she whispered. "I don't think she'd care if you looked at her a bit, though."

Samuel put the mug down on the table and went to stand next to Elizabeth. He crossed his arms over his chest, giving the distinct impression that he wasn't in a mood for any funny business. *Try messing with Grete,* he appeared to be saying, *and I'll mess you about before you get a chance.*

"She's awful pale," Luke whispered, and several of the other children nodded.

"Hope they put honey in her tea," another one added. "It goes down better with honey."

After a few minutes, Isabelle motioned everyone outside. They gathered on the porch. Isabelle glanced around. All the sticks were gone. When she looked at Jacob, he winked and nodded toward the side of the house.

"Do you believe me now, that she's not a witch?" Isabelle asked the kids gathered around her. "That real witches don't need people like Hen and me to nurse them back to health?"

Most of them nodded. Isabelle looked at Elizabeth and was surprised to see she had tears in her eyes.

"Wish someone had been there for my mam," the girl whispered. "But no one would come. They didn't want to get what she had. Only Da would help, and he died too."

Sugar walked across the porch and stood next to Elizabeth. "Grete's not a witch, you know," she said. "You shouldn't have told everyone to bring sticks."

Elizabeth swiped her hand across her eyes. "I thought it would help, having her dead."

"It wouldn't have, though," said Sugar.

"No," Elizabeth agreed. "It wouldn't have."

"Why don't you all sit down, and I'll fix us some breakfast?" Isabelle suggested, and the children settled themselves on the porch, in the rockers, and on the steps. Turning to go inside, she was surprised to find Jacob on her heels. "What are you doing?"

"I'll help ya with breakfast," Jacob told her. "I'm good in the kitchen. Just ask Grete in there."

Isabelle closed her eyes. Laugh or cry? How to choose?

She took a deep breath, shook her head.

She laughed.

Lemon balm (*Melissa officinalis*)

Soothes the aching head,
calms the quick heart,
gentles the aching gut.

42

It was decided they would have lemon balm soup for lunch, and it was further decided that Isabelle would gather the lemon balm, just to prove she could.

"She'll learn yet," Grete said, leaning over to the woman in the rocking chair next to her on the porch. "Not everyone's like your Hen, practically born knowing."

The woman nodded but didn't reply. Isabelle admired how Grete was taking her time with Hen's mother—Dreama—pointing out in quiet ways that Hen had gifts that shouldn't go to waste. Hen's mother never said anything other than "Aye" or "Is that so?" in response, if she responded at all, but

Isabelle thought she could see the seeds Grete was planting slowly taking root in Dreama's mind.

Isabelle set out toward the back of the cottage, to the shady patch behind the woodpile. Lemon balm, unlike most herbs, she'd learned during her nightly studies, could flourish in the shade, and Isabelle thought she knew where a clump of it might be growing.

In the three weeks since the night Grete almost died, Isabelle had become a studier of plants, a student of botany, a one-woman memorizer of every herb that ever bloomed, just as she'd promised herself she would. True, she lacked Hen's natural talents, and after a half hour or so of reading about sneezeweed or moneywort or sweet woodruff, her eyes grew heavy and drool collected on the pages of the books Grete had given her to study. But Isabelle was determined. She could learn this stuff.

She found the patch of lemon balm where she remembered it to be and began gently extracting leaves from the stems and placing them in her basket. Lemon balm had a minty scent that Isabelle found exceedingly pleasant. Maybe her job here would be to garden. Grete was so weak now, she would definitely need help digging and weeding and planting new plants in the spring, collecting seeds from the plants in the fall. Isabelle the Gardener. It had a nice ring.

First, though, the lemon balm, and then the making of the soup. Well, Jacob would want to do that, and Isabelle guessed that would be okay, even though right now her mission was to be indispensable, and what was more indispensable than someone who could make a delicious bowl of soup? Besides, after the poisoning, could you really trust Jacob by himself in the kitchen? But he would insist, trying as hard as he could to make up for almost killing Grete.

Hen called to Isabelle from the kitchen as she walked inside with the basket of leaves. "Mam says we'll be going after lunch. She doesn't want to leave Callou watching the wee ones too long, and besides, there's chores to be done."

"You want to go down to the creek tomorrow?"

Isabelle asked as she laid the basket down on the counter by the sink. "I need to start learning about mushrooms."

"If there's time," Hen replied. "Grete has some packages she needs to be made up. There's a rough cough going round in the village."

Isabelle began rinsing off the herbs. Maybe Jacob wouldn't want to cook today, and she could have the job to herself. She needed to prove herself necessary, useful, a part of the big picture.

She could still see Grete's face when Isabelle had told her the night before what she'd decided: She wasn't going back to the other world. Grete's left eyebrow had risen up halfway to her hairline, as though she wondered at the wisdom of Isabelle's decision.

"You sure you wouldn't miss your mother, girl?" she'd asked, readjusting the blanket on her lap so that it more fully covered her knees. "And that she wouldn't be missing you if you never returned?"

"I'd miss her," Isabelle had said plainly, already regretting that she wouldn't be able to tell her mother that she was a changeling and potentially a magical being. "But I think you need me more than she does."

"Hmmm," had been Grete's murmured reply, and Isabelle hadn't pressed the matter further. She had armloads of arguments she'd reasoned out each night in bed, how Grete was old and weak now and needed her help. If she went back, who would cook for Grete? Tend to her herbs, dry them and package them? Hen and Jacob would help, but for how long?

Besides, maybe Isabelle could go home later, when Grete was better, steadier on her feet. Maybe by then she'd have figured out the tricks for moving back and forth between the two worlds. Maybe she could bring her mom back with her. Family reunion!

The fact was, Isabelle couldn't bear to let Grete out of her sight for long. The palms of her hands got clammy and her legs started to itch.

"I've got a balm that will fix that," said Grete when Isabelle confessed it made her nervous to be away from her. "Settle you right down."

"I'll settle down when I see you totally and completely well," Isabelle told her grandmother.

"That will take some time, girl," Grete told her. "And all the while your life is passing you by, and your mother's, too."

But Isabelle stood firm. She would stay. Grete needed her.

She carried the lemon balm to the cutting board and began to chop the stems into small pieces she would simmer for the soup. As if by magic, Jacob appeared at her side. "Let me do that," he said, reaching for the knife. "Grete says she needs you on the porch."

Isabelle wiped her hands on a rag and went outside. Hen's mother was standing as though ready to go. "I want to send Hen and Dreama home with some nice spring potatoes," Grete told Isabelle. "I've got a basket in the cellar, more than you and I can eat before they begin to sprout."

Isabelle started to frown—she'd rather cook than haul loads of potatoes—but quickly turned up the corners of her mouth. She was Isabelle the Useful and Necessary, and she would do what she was told, even if only two days earlier Hen had found a black snake curled in the corner of the cellar catching a nap.

The cellar was cool and smelled vaguely like a laundry room—damp and earthy and clean in spite of itself. The door clicked closed behind her as Isabelle carefully made her way down the rickety steps. She reached for a light switch and then remembered that she was in a land without light switches or electricity or Animal Control people who would come round up errant snakes from the basement upon request. Holding on to the railing, she felt each step with her toe before putting her whole foot down.

The cellar was dimly lit by light streaming through a small window. Ah, there were the potatoes, basking in a little spot of sun in the middle of the room, and not a snake to be seen. Isabelle breathed a sigh of relief and hoisted the basket to her hip. She held again to the railing and made her way up the steps. Balancing carefully on the top step, she reached out and twisted the doorknob.

It was stuck.

Do not get irritated, Isabelle told herself, trying the doorknob again. *Be cheerful. Everyone loves a cheerful girl with a basket full of potatoes.* The doorknob refused to budge. She tried it again. No luck.

She knocked on the door. "Jacob! Hen! The door is stuck!"

Nothing.

The darkness from the basement's dim corners began to creep up the steps behind her. The floor issued a slight hissing noise (or so it seemed to Isabelle), as though not just one snake but a whole battery of snakes had gathered at the foot of the stairs.

Isabelle dropped the basket and pounded at the door. "Let me out of here!" she yelled, not caring any longer if she sounded irritable or angry or unpleasant. "Please, somebody, let me out!"

And then: The door opened.

Isabelle let out a sigh of relief. "Thank goodness," she said—

—and Isabelle Bean fell back out.

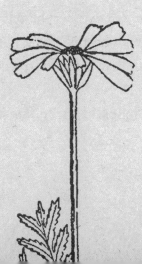

43

"I'm sorry, Isabelle, jeez! I was just joking around!"

Charley Bender stood in front of the nurse's closet, a look of dismay on her face. "Are you scared of the dark? I totally apologize if you are. Really, it was just a joke. And you were only in there for, like, five seconds."

Five seconds?

Isabelle took a deep breath before exiting the closet. She needed to collect herself. She didn't want to cry. She was sure this was a mistake after all, a silly blip that Grete could fix, no problem—

Five seconds?

"I'm okay," she said finally. "I'm just a little claustrophobic."

Charley sat down at the nurse's desk and rested her foot on the edge of the trash can. "Oh, me too. My friend Deirdre has this bathroom in her basement that's maybe the size of a refrigerator. I can't make myself use it. I start getting hives."

Isabelle sat down in the chair next to the door. She needed to steady herself, to readjust. She looked down at her feet and saw that her red boots were as shiny as they'd been when she first fell in.

And then, beneath the soles, she felt the buzz again. Was it coming from down below? Was Grete calling her back? Was something wrong, somebody sick? Was the buzz coming from the camps? But how could that be? The kids had all gone home.

No, Isabelle realized, looking across the room.

It was coming from Charley Bender.

"How's your ankle?" asked Isabelle. Even from where she sat, she could see the swelling underneath Charley's sock.

"It hurts," Charley admitted. "It hurts a lot."

"I could get you some ice from the cafeteria,"

Isabelle offered. She stood up. "It would probably take down the swelling."

"That would be great." Charley sounded grateful, and Isabelle noticed there were tears just beneath the surface of her voice. "I don't know if that nurse is ever going to get here."

"I kind of know a lot about first aid," Isabelle told her. "My grandmother taught me."

"All my grandmother ever taught me was to play bridge." Charley smiled at Isabelle. "Pretty boring."

Isabelle nodded. "I'll be right back."

She left the nurse's office and turned in the direction of the cafeteria. As she walked down the long corridor, thoughts drifted out into the hallway from underneath doorways and followed her. Isabelle could feel them coming up from behind. She could make out bits and pieces of words. She knew she had a lot of work to do.

Maybe she wouldn't have time to miss everything she'd left behind.

I still hear children's thoughts from time to time, but mostly it's Grete's thoughts I hear, old woman thoughts, arthritic thoughts, thoughts that think they're forty years younger than they actually are. She needs help weeding the garden or putting together a packet of goldenseal powder, and it distresses her that she can't do her job as well as she used to. I hear the distress, and then it stops. That's when I know Hen has arrived.

I wish I could hear Hen's and Samuel's thoughts, but I can't. I'm a half changeling. My gifts are limited.

In fact, I'm afraid they're fading into nothingness.

So, yes, you've probably seen me and my mom, a

relatively normal pair, a woman nearing sixty and her daughter about to graduate from high school, a little strange-looking, maybe, a silver strand of other-worldliness barely visible along their spines, but nothing too out of the ordinary about either of us as we walk through town and knock on doors, pull on the handles, poke our heads hopefully inside.

It was hard at first to convince my mom to come look, as you might imagine. It took some doing. A lot of storytelling. This story, as a matter of fact.

My mother, the changeling. When I came back from the other world, I clung to her like a dryer sheet to the back of a nylon blouse. I examined her top to toe, interpreted the constellations of freckles on her arms, hid in closets and behind doors, just to see if she'd do anything odd or even magic (maybe fairy dust had rubbed off on her when she'd been stolen; you never could tell).

It turned out that for the most part, my mother was just a mom, a stressed-out mom who worried she didn't know what she was doing, a mother who'd never been mothered herself, or been a daughter for that matter.

But: Once, a few months after I'd come back, I cut my arm on an exposed nail—it was a light cut, a ribbon of red, the blood barely rising from the skin—and my mother put her hand over the wound—

And the cut disappeared.

True story.

"Put your hand over mine," I told her the first time I took her to the nurse's office. "And believe. Just believe for five seconds. That's all it will take."

It didn't work. Is it because my mother doesn't really believe? Or is it because I'm getting too old, too practical, too mature?

Anyway, I was thinking . . .

Maybe you could help me?

The doors are out there. If you could just twist a few out-of-the-way doorknobs, check the custodian's closet at your school, pay attention to the ground under the soles of your shoes—

If you feel a buzz beneath your toes, let me know.

FIGHTING GREEK GODS.
SAVING THE WORLD.
GETTING TOTALLY GROUNDED.

Book One:
The Shadow Thieves

Book Two:
The Siren Song

Book Three:
The Immortal Fire